•

Two Willow Chairs

•

Two Willow Chairs

Short Fiction
by Jess Wells

Library B Books
San Francisco

Dedicated with much love and respect to my mother, Jeanette

Also by Jess Wells

Run, 1981

The Sharda Stories, 1982

A Herstory of Prostitution in Western Europe
(Shameless Hussy Press, Oakland, Calif.), 1982

The Dress, The Cry and A Shirt With No Seams,
first edition, copyright 1984
second edition, copyright 1985

The Dress/The Sharda Stories,
re-edited and revised, first edition by
Library B Books, 1986

Stories in this volume have appeared in
Common Lives/Lesbian Lives, Womantide, and *When I Am An
Old Woman I Shall Wear Purple* (Papier Mache Press)

Book Design and Cover Illustration by Tim Barrett,
Studio de Boom
Jacket Photo: Helen Keller
Desktop Publishing by The Laser Edge
Printing by BookCrafters

Library B Books
584 Castro #224
San Francisco, CA 94114

ACKNOWLEDGEMENTS

I'm lousy in the eleventh hour, those moments for profound airport good-byes, spaces for the description of myself at the end of anthologies, the 'heartfelt' feelings that go into these spaces called acknowledgements. For perhaps the first time, however, I have a broad support system of people whose generosity requires my thanks. First and foremost I thank Sharon Aurora, the woman who has shown me true partnership, who loves me and encourages me with health, devotion and honesty. Into my life she brings her two daughters, Kristie Aurora and Laurie Schimmelman, women I feel blessed to know and love. I take this time and space to thank the long-standing loyalty of Barbara Le-Vine and Ralle Greenburg, and to praise the meticulous, perceptive editing ability of Laurie E. Werbner, as well as the flattering camera's eye of Helen Keller. To Tim Barrett, what fun to watch the growth of a professional language. Thanks go to Kate Millett, Sandy Boucher, Judy Grahn and Sarah Schulman, Carol Seajay and the members of my Women's Success Team. Many thanks to my blood family, who must wonder if I am analyzing them at every moment (I am not) and when I will ever write something they could leave on the coffee table. Thanks go to my brother Craig and sister-in-law Debbie for coming back into my life and bringing Lauren Ashley with them. Lastly, devotions to Tara, who reminds me that ultimately, it is she and I in this little vessel crossing the waters.

C O N T E N T S

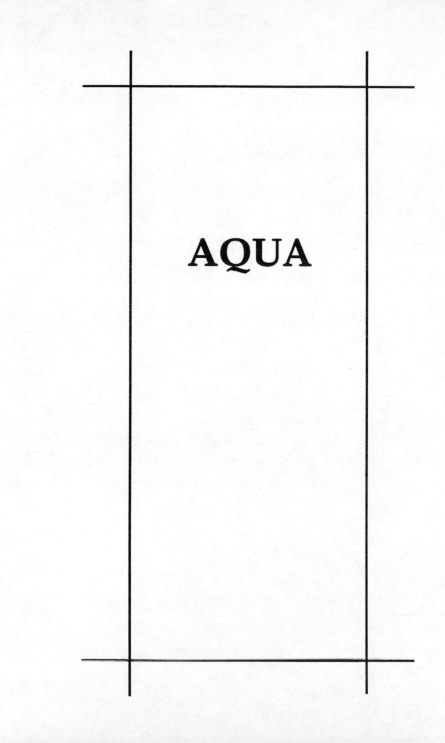

AQUA

● AQUA

I'd never seen anyone looking so relaxed and content, her cowgirl boots propped on a chair-back, face pointing up to the blistering sky as if waiting for a kiss. Her jeans were tight, her shirt unbuttoned to the middle of her chest and she was so long and stretched out that I didn't want to disturb her but I had car trouble and in the middle of the desert you don't have many choices.

"'Scuse me," I said, stepping onto the wooden porch. "Wouldn't you know this piece of junk'd be having problems and me in the middle of nowhere with no money and nobody to call. I don't suppose you'd have any ideas, would you?"

I didn't have any reason to be explaining my financial business to this woman but somehow my mouth forgot all about privacy that day. I should have seen from the response I got that it was time to back off the porch and leave. She slowly turned her head and opened her eyes, little green slits in a face that had been taut for the sun, but was now wrinkled and parched as it surveyed a sweaty traveler on the steps. I know not to poke at spiders, even the harmless ones, but I proceeded anyway.

"My car's acting up. Is there a station near here...or a phone?"

"Nope. Neither of those but you can sit down if you want. We got a birthday party here," and she turned her face back to the sun.

I crossed the eight-foot porch, stood at the wooden chair beside her.

"But don't sit on the hat," she mumbled.

I scowled at her.

"You know about cars?" I asked, picking up the cowgirl hat and, finding no place suitable for such a gem, snapped it into her lap. I sat. She turned, sensing the challenge and plopped her hat on one of the railing posts.

"What's the trouble?"

"I'm losing power. She's not good for much, this car, but every few minutes she gets slower and more tired, then she picks up speed again."

"It's from the heat."

No joke, I thought. I considered leaving, trying to ignore how worried I was about the car or how much I hoped she'd offer me something to drink. Everything was from the heat, as if the sun were making us all water drops in an oily skillet. Everyone I had talked to today was irritable and short, things popping out of their mouths that belonged miles away from their minds. How she could sit there staring up at the sun was more than I could gather. I was ready to dash into her house uninvited and drink anything I could find.

"Park it behind the house to cool down. Relax. She'll be alright after the sun goes down a bit. Your radiator alright?"

"I don't know. I'd be surprised if it was. Whose birthday?"

She took her feet down and turned to me, stroking sun-blond hair from her forehead. "Sorry, I'm not really unfriendly. I get like a lizard in this heat—just bake in

the sun and forget everything. It's mine. My birthday."
She got up and went into the house.

"Congratulations! So, do you live here year
'round?" I called after her.

"Yeah. You want some ginger ale? It's all the
party favors I got."

"Love it. What is it today, 95, 100 degrees?" I
asked, feeling the sweat running down my cleavage.

"Hundred and two," she handed me a tall glass
with ice and bubbly, the refrigerator in the house moaning
against the battle of being opened. The ice shattered and
scurried around in my glass as I took a long swallow.

"You traveling alone?" She stretched out and
looked straight ahead, the lines in her face deep and dry.

"Always."

She grunted her approval.

"My name's Jody. Thanks for this," I said, salut-
ing her with the half-empty glass. "So where's all the party
guests? Am I the first?"

"My name's Aqua," she toasted without looking
away from the sun.

"That's your name? I mean, aren't you a little far
from home?" I laughed. I should have quit right then, I
know that now, but the porch was shady where I was sitting and I would have pawed the ground for another glass
of ginger ale.

"I was thinking about that just as you came up, actually." She turned to me. "Born in the sea. No point in
staying."

"No point...?" I muttered. Looking back on the
day, I can see what I was doing: picking and poking, bear-
ing down like the sun had been doing on me all day.

"I told you," she was getting annoyed. "I was born
there. You know," her voice went low and conspiratorial,
"it's like trying to stay in your momma forever."

Dyke, I thought. Our eyes met. Only a dyke calls
a car 'she' and talks about being born.

5

"I like the ocean, actually. The breeze, the smell of it, the constant pounding..." I said, confused, wishing the ocean would pour around my miserable body instead of this puddle of sweat sitting on the shelf of my belly and this sand chafing the back of my neck. "I'm talkin' about a nice cool dip in the water."

"I hate the ocean," she said brusquely. "Had enough of it, anyway, that's for sure." She leapt out of her seat, alive suddenly, her mind waking up, her energy running up and down her long body in a torrent.

"Think your car's cooled down," she said through clenched teeth. "We could check her radiator. Maybe tighten a few belts." She went into the house for another ginger ale. "Never mind. You still thirsty?" I followed her.

"Yeah."

"How about bourbon in this one?"

I nodded.

"Oh, now I'm coming alive. Christ, who can think in that sun. Besides, I don't get a lot of company—not many women travel alone and even fewer come through here." She handed me my glass and looked at me. "Not women like you, anyway."

"Like us, you mean?" I said. She just snorted, stared into her bourbon with a splash of ginger ale. "Whaddaya do out here— for work, I mean?" I said.

"I'm a dancer in Reno. One of the big clubs—not strip, mind you, I'm a dancer. I throw everything I've got into every piece of music, so I'm good."

"Sounds great, Aqua," I said in a lack-luster tone. There was something missing in the way she said it, like a birthday party with no guests.

"It's life to me, you know, the joy and beauty of it all, set to music. I tell 'ya, Jody," she said, with a dead-pan face, "there's nothing like it. Life just leapin' and jumpin' all over the place. Hey, bottom's up."

"To life," I said.

"Yeah. I'll go for that. And you? You gotta work?"

"I work with kids. Preschool in San Francisco."

"Oh, now, that must be something. Little ones. Damn'd if life isn't glorious, you know?" She smiled but her eyes never changed, still little green slits with no sparkle.

"Most of the time, I suppose," I said, looking into my glass.

"Ah, all the time, honey. Just when things get bad at work, somebody gives me attitude or the place gets so smoky it makes me sick, well, just then I'll be driving home, tied up in knots, and there's the sun rising and it looks so...so," and she blew a half-kiss to the air, trying to explain joy to me with the broken face of someone watching their only chance at love drive away.

"You know what I mean?" she said.

"It must be really beautiful around here," I said, following her back outdoors.

"Oh, it is. I love the dust and the sun and the way the wind smells so dry out here. People think just because the sun shines all the time that the weather's always the same but they're crazy. There's spring sun different from winter sun and the flowers—you really have to know where to look to see them. Cactus, birds, the clouds. And the hills? They're solid rock and they look different, too. Even the dunes—you saw them a couple of miles south, right?"

"Yeah. Beautiful."

"All the tourists go to the dunes. Well even *they* have seasons and there ain't nothin' grows out there." She took a long swallow. "Flowers are just a lazy way to tell the seasons, anyway.

"Makes me happy to think all this grows without water."

I looked at her with a long and steady gaze until she turned to me and her face seemed to close up again. She reached down and pulled at my glass.

"Time for a refill."

I shrugged my shoulders and let her take my glass back into the house.

"We got a little party goin' on here, huh?" she called, dropping in more ice. "Well, good," she kicked the screen door open and handed my glass over my shoulder. "I don't drink, really. I've had this bottle for a long time, but what the hell. Today's my birthday and...it's nice to have company."

"So Happy Birthday," I said, raising my glass. "How old are you?"

"Sixteen," she said, flopping into her chair. I laughed.

"So when did *you* stop counting."

"I said, I'm 16," she leaned over the arm of her chair, grave and threatening.

"Well, you don't *look* 16," I said, trying to diffuse the situation by touching the deep crows-feet around her eyes.

"Hey," she pulled away violently. "I said there weren't *many* of you women traveling through, I didn't say there weren't *any*."

"Sorry," I said, setting my glass on the chair and holding up passive hands.

"Yeah, well, I'd say you should keep that glass between your legs, girl."

"Is that so? Well, I imagine you'd be as frosty if you were there."

"Oooh, now, I don't have to be this friendly. You could just get in your car and scald, you know." She plopped her feet on the railing, then sighed and turned back to me.

"Oh, I'm sorry," she said, shaking her head. "But damnit, it's my birthday. Sixteen years ago I was born from the sea."

"Aqua," I said, feeling brave from the drink.

"Alright, alright. It's the anniversary of my mother's death," she said, lowering her voice. "You want another drink?" She got up, quite drunk now and groped into the house, came back with both bottles under her arms. "Save some energy and just bring 'um out here, hell."

"I'm sorry about your mother," I said softly, fearing thin ice.

"What for?" she asked, quietly, twisting open the ginger ale. "She had a choice."

"She killed herself?" I felt sick inside, knowing I was prodding a lizard that had hissed its last warning.

"Yep. She sure did. Nearly killed me and my little sister with her. Did kill my little sister."

She wiped sweat from her forehead with her sleeve. "I shouldn't be so hard on her, I suppose. She had a bad time of it. Two kids, one always sick—my sister was such a weak little thing—and no man around, though when he was, it was worse than when he wasn't of course. She was a grill cook. We lived in a little town by the ocean. You know, same old story."

"Work to pay the bills but the ends don't meet so you work some more and they still don't meet?" I asked sympathetically.

"Yeah. Well, one day she couldn't do it anymore so she put on her best sweater and pants, strapped my sister to her chest with the tablecloth and grabbed me by the wrist. Marched us on down to the sea. You don't want to hear this."

"Well...I do if you want to tell it," I said cautiously.

"She stood there for hours, looking at the water and nothing could move her. Her face didn't change. Not once. I know 'cause I watched her. I think maybe she'd taken a bunch of pills or something because I've never seen anybody so unreachable, you know, their face miles behind their flesh. So, we're standin' on this cliff and I keep going "c'mon Mom, let's go home now. What's the matter, Mom? We better go—you gotta cook in the morning." She looked down at her boots, then out towards the desert. "Well, Happy Birthday Aqua.

"I guess I was about eight, ten. Anyway, she never looked at me, just all of a sudden hiked me onto her back and dove off the cliff onto the rocks."

"Jesus Christ," I said, setting my glass onto the porch.

"Oh now, don't go all dramatic on me. It was a short cliff. Maybe about six feet up. Can you believe that? I mean, why'd she pick a place like that? My little sister, she died right away. She didn't know what was going on and she sure was too small to make up her own mind, but me, I clung to the back of that sweater like it was the edge of the world. I guess when we hit, I rolled off and I just lay there, on the top of the rocks."

"Oh Aqua, I'm really sorry."

"Real flat ones, like shelves out into the water, with crevices running through them. So I'm flat on my belly—I didn't want to look towards Mom, and I was thinking, 'You better hurry up and die before the tide comes in.'" She snorted, taking another long pull on her drink. "Pretty weird, huh?"

Aqua got up from where she was slumped over in her chair and walked to the end of the porch, leaning her forearms on the railing and kicking at the sand piled up around the posts. She finished her drink and poured another.

"I remember everything—every single thing— about that night. It's like I can still feel the stone against my belly and the coldness. Must be because it's my birthday but I can see that water surging up, waving the green slime back and forth, saying, 'get out'a here girl, leave *now*, you've seen enough, now go!'

"It started gettin' dark so I got up and didn't ever look over at my mother, I just went straight to the cafe and told 'em what happened and they took me in. Mrs. Miller put me in her house behind the cafe and put me to work washing dishes but I don't remember much about being there. It's like my mind went blank until the day I ran away and swore I'd celebrate life always." Aqua strode across the porch and clinked glasses with me. "Yes m'am. Celebrate.

"Oh hell, there, traveler Jody, don't look so sad-faced," she laughed with a crooked smile, quite drunk. "Everybody makes their choices: she chose to die and I chose to live and that's that. No regrets, goddamnit," she said, pouring another drink into her half-full glass. "I say life's burden enough without carrying around a lot of sadness. Here's to it, honey—lightening life's burden. To dancing!"

The sun was finally going down and the desert was lit up behind her. As Aqua leaned on the railing, she looked on fire like the sand.

"Mamba, rumba, salza," she twisted and spun in her boots, laughing with her mouth but her eyes still tiny and expressionless. "And of course square dancing and the two-step: I even know Czechoslovakian folk dances—pretty, real pretty. You should come see me dance, Jody."

"Great. I'd...like that a lot," I said, heavy and frightened.

She yanked open the screen door with a laugh and stumbled inside, turning on lights. I followed her into the tiny house and went to the sink to rinse out my glass. I'd had half the number that she had downed but another drink and I'd never be able to drive: I was already counting on the freeway being a straight away through the desert. I turned on the water, feeling it cool and refreshing across my wrists.

"What are you doing?" Aqua said, alarmed.

"You don't have to play hostess, I can..."

"Turn off the water!"

"What?"

"Turn it off!" she shouted, stumbling across the cabin towards me. "I don't like it...water...in my house. It...makes the place smell."

I turned to Aqua, who was deliriously drunk, leaning over the back of a chair, looking down at the plastic-covered kitchen table.

"Damp. I hate it. Everything was so damp, Jody, my little bed behind the cafe, the air every day. Every single fucking day was wet," she said, and I, parched despite the drinks, standing there gritty and sandy and covered with dried sweat, looked at her as if she were talking about the moon.

"The salt all over my body from lying in the water, the lichen...in my nose, on my cheeks, green and...wet. Little...things swimming in the tide pools." She turned her head in disgust and staggered backwards. I wiped my hands on my dusty pants and grabbed her by the shoulders, leading her to her iron cot against the wall where she slumped onto her side, face twisted and closed, knees to her chest, hands like dried claws. I grabbed one of her feet to take off her boots.

"I swear to you, I can still feel it, Jody. Her sweater."

I took off her boots, and as the sand poured out onto the floor I looked at this woman, all parched skin and rough hands, passed out in her dusty house. I thought of my own mother, baking cakes she never ate, wringing her hands while she stared out the windows at nothing, and I knew there was no running from the pain of knowing that your mother may never be happy. I set the boots beside her and fished in my pockets for the keys. Feeling helpless and withered, I quietly closed the screen door behind me and, touching the sand on the railing as if willing it to protect her, I got in my car and drove.

TWO
WILLOW
CHAIRS

•

TWO
WILLOW
CHAIRS

This is a lesbian portrait, I tell my friends, pointing at the photo in a silver frame on my desk, but they don't understand. To them, it's just a snapshot of two empty chairs, and they cock their heads at me, wondering why the photo has a place of honor and the chairs are the subject of such elaborate plans.

I took the picture when I was 17, which made the chairs brand new, my mother's sister Ruth and her lover Florence in their fifties, and their relationship in its fifteenth year. Flo's chair is made of willow branches, twisted into locking half moons, a rugged chair that somehow looks like filigree. Next to it on their lawn—a secluded, overgrown stretch of grass and overhanging vines—is Ruth's willow chair, a simpler one with a broad seat and armrests that circle like a hug. All around the chairs are flower beds, usually gone to seed, and grass that was "never properly cut," my step-father would growl in the car on the way home from visits, grass thick like fur that Flo would wiggle her toes in, digging into the peat until her feet were black and she would hide them inside their slippers again.

The year of this snapshot, Aunt Florence was "struck with spring" as she used to say to me. We arrived on the Fourth of July to find blooming peonies and iris and marigold ("always marigold against the snails," she would whisper to me, as if imparting the wisdom of womanhood). Florence and my mother wandered the garden, pointing at stalks and talking potting soil, promising cuttings to each other and examining the grape vines up the trellis, while Ruth and my step-father faced each other silently, she slumped in the willow chair like a crest-fallen rag doll and he sitting rigid, twisted sideways on the plastic webbing of a broken chrome chair. I wandered the yard alone with the garden hose. After ten minutes of listening to the women's voices but not hearing anything, Ruth got up and slouched into the house to start bringing out the beers, calling in an overly- loud voice, "So, Dick (everyone else called him Richard), "how's business?"

Talking commerce was a great diversion for him, and my mother was already occupied with explaining her begonias, which left me to be the only one in the place grappling with the realization that this lesbian child was being deposited for the summer with the family's lesbian aunts because a new step-father, two brothers and a male cat were more than I could possibly stand. It was the first of many such summers, visits that after a few years turned into summers with autumns and then special Christmases and soon all important holidays and all important matters of any kind. That first summer, nervously pacing the backyard, I knew it would develop into this and when my parents finally left, Ruth and Florence and I stared at each other with wonderment. They'd never had a family before and all of a sudden they had a daughter, full-grown and up in their faces feeling awkward. Since my mother was straight, there was something I could dismiss about her, but here were these two, with the weight of maturity *and* the righteousness of twenty years of lesbian lifestyle behind them. Now *that's* what I considered authority.

Aunt Ruth breathed a sigh of relief after the car had pulled out of the drive. Florence let some of her gaiety drop but turned to me, ready to fulfill her last social obligation of the day.

"Beetle," as she had called me since the time I was a baby with big eyes, "Welcome." There was so much hesitancy in her voice, fear almost, as if this child, who did not really know about being a lesbian, were looking at a lesbian who did not really know about being in a family. I dropped the garden hose and wiped my hands on my pants, trying to smooth my carrot-red hair that was frizzy in six different directions. Florence strode over and gathered me in her arms.

"I don't know about these chairs," Ruth said, getting up and yanking one out of the grass. "Let's take them back by the trellis," she said to me, "Florence's favorite spot." And we all grabbed chairs, me taking my mother's chrome one since it was known to all but Richard that his was the only broken chair in the place. We settled into the afternoon, our conversation picking up pace while Florence shuttled lemonade and beers. That's when I got my first photo of the chairs.

Ruth was sitting sideways, her leg slung over the arm of the chair, head thrown back, her whole big body lit by a streak of afternoon sun. Florence was struck by spring only in selected places, and the back of the yard was not one of them: the grape vines behind Ruth's head dangled low and free, the grass crept up around her chair even though it was early in the season.

We had become very quiet for a moment and Ruth turned in her chair to talk privately to Florence. My camera caught her in mid-sentence, her mouth open, hand reaching for her lover's knee, her eyes still not aware that Aunt Flo was in the house and that she and I were alone. Her face showed all the tenderness, history, trust in her femme as she turned to ask, "Wren, what was the name of that..."

Ruth looked back at me. "I wish you'd quit with that camera," she growled weakly as I laid the photo on the tops of the tall grass to develop, already sensing that I had exposed her. And in a way, she was right. Until then, I had used this camera as a form of self-defense, silently proving to my brothers that they looked stupid, threatening to catch them in the act, snapping photos of my mother as if to prove to myself that she wasn't just a phantom woman. But this day, this photo of Ruth and the empty willow chair was the first photo I had ever taken in an attempt to preserve something beautiful.

I handed the photo to Florence first as she returned with two beers and a lemonade. She stared at it a long time, seeing the look on Ruth's face.

"Oh God, Wren, get rid of that! I look like a jerk," Ruth protested, but Florence held the photo close to her.

"You look wonderful. Besides, I want a photo of my chairs. Here Beetle, take a picture of the chairs for me. Rudy, get up. God, I wish the garden looked better."

Florence kept the two photos in her jewelry box for years. The two willow chairs stayed in their places in the back of the yard and whenever I would visit (on leave from the Army, or home from another city) we would first convene at the chairs, even during the winter when we would huddle in big coats, and share important news like a ritual before rushing inside for the evening.

Years later, when Florence gave the photos to me, there was one taken of myself and Flo sitting on a porch step, our pant legs rolled up from gathering mussels in the tidepools. Florence is gesturing to me, her arms in the shape of a bowl.

"Now look, honey," she said that day, "don't give up. Love is just a matter of the right recipe: a cup and a half of infatuation, a pinch of matching class status, two tablespoons of compatible politics and three generous cups of good sex. Mix. Sprinkle liberally with the ability to communicate and fold into a well-greased and floured apartment. You bake it for at least six months without slamming the door and pray you have love in the morning. And it works—when you've got the right ingredients."

Of course their relationship was a serious one, so I have photos of times when the recipe wasn't quite right with the two of them, either. In the package with the other photos is a black and white from the 50's of Florence in a wool suit and a hat with a veil, standing at the rail of an ocean-liner. She and Ruth put all the money they had into a ticket for her to go to Europe and even though it was the best trip she'd ever taken, she looks miserable in the picture. The veil is down over her face, almost to her lips that are thick with lipstick, and she's wearing kidskin gloves but not waving. She looks very tight and cold to me in this picture, but Ruth liked how smart Flo looked. Aunt Florence would stand in front of it, holding my hand (even though I was home on leave for the third and last year) and say, "Beetle, I keep it because it reminds me of when I was less frightened of running and being alone than of staying and loving." She turned to me, one hand on her hip. "Now isn't that ridiculous, to think that it's less scary to have a lousy relationship than a good one? That intimacy is more terrifying than loneliness. God, the world is so crazy, Beetle. It's like saying garbage is more delectable than food." Well, I stood in front of that photo with her, looking up at her glowing face, then back at the picture of that sunken young thing and it seemed her face now wasn't wrinkled by age, just stretched from being so open. I thought about my latest crush in the barracks and how good Florence's choice seems to have been (after all, here was home and warmth and Ruth lounging on the sofa throwing cashews to the dog), but I looked back at that picture, those eyes big and scared and I knew that's where I was, a veil over *my* face. I turned from my aunt and thought, 'Oh Jesus, somebody send me a ticket and point me towards the ocean.'

Ruth kept the photo at her side of the bed, as if to remind herself of how far Florence had run and how close she now lived.

On Florence's side of the bed was a photo taken the summer after she returned. The two are in funny brown swimsuits with pointed bras, Ruth sleeping in Florence's arms. Flo is bending to kiss her on the neck and years later, she related to me that, lying in the sand with her lover in her arms, Florence could feel the years passing. She could feel Ruth getting older even though she was in her thirties, feel her getting heavier through middle age, belly growing across her hips, feel her shift in her sleep from an injury to her shoulder that she didn't have yet, see the scars she would have in the future, Ruth getting smaller and more frail as she aged, wrinkling into buttery skin. And all the time, holding Ruth encircled in her arms, Florence knew that this would be the progress of her world, that this was her future and her life, that this woman between her arms was her home.

Of course Flo had pictures of her Mom and Dad, who have been dead for nearly two decades now, and the family at picnics, Ruth playing horseshoes on her sixtieth birthday and pictures of me when I was a kid with teeth missing, though we won't go into that. There's another lesbian portrait in this stack from Flo— it's a picture of a dog.

Clarise was the spaniel Florence had when she was lovers with the woman before Ruth (which is how she was always referred to, she never had a name) and Flo kept the photo on top of the television for years after she had left the woman and the dog. The little thing was sitting attentively on the beach, clumps of dirt hanging on its paws. It was the first dog Florence had ever learned to love, and every year, with a far-away look in her eyes, Flo would ramble on about how special and psychic and beautiful and protective it was. It was everything a dog should be. Just a few years ago, Ruth, sick and lying on the couch, threw off the afghan and snatched the photo off the t.v.

"For Godsake, Florence, it's over, and it's okay that it's over," she shouted, starting to cough. "The dog wasn't the only thing good and the woman wasn't the only thing bad. Now c'mon."

Florence went into the back yard and sat in her willow chair. It was her 70th birthday and she should have a jacket on, I thought.

"Stay here, Beetle," Ruth said.

"I don't see why you're jealous of a dog, Rudy. For Christsake, it was years ago."

"I'm not jealous. Florence doesn't know what to do with all those years she spent with that woman and so she puts them here," she said, tapping the glass frame. "When you're consumed with bitterness, where do you put all the good times? The dog. The only reason I'm even saying it is because she knows it herself. A couple of months ago, we went to Bolinas, remember the spot...?"

"Where we used to gather mussels?"

"Right. Well, Wren thought the air would make me feel better or something, but who should come trotting up but the spitting image of that dog. Splatters mud all over Wren's newspaper, knocks the damn iced tea into the potato chips and rolls over to stick up her tits, I mean it. Well, it finally dawns on Wren, 'Goddamn, maybe that Clarise was just a fucking dog, too.'"

Now I have the photo of Clarise. I keep it with a bunch of others Florence gave me in a white, unmarked envelope. These are the painful pictures, the ones that bring floods of heat to your face, pictures you look at and smell perfume.

There's a picture of Florence pointing at the flowerbeds with her cane, trying to get *me* to be struck with spring and do some planting while we waited for Ruth to get well. Then there's Ruth lying on the couch covered with the afghan, looking tiny and angry, and after Ruth died, a photo of Florence looking remarkably like her picture in the hat with the veil. Florence never went back to the chairs, never went into the back of the yard, only stared at it from the kitchen window, stricken now that Ruth, love, hope and future were dead and decaying, confused by the sight of the grass and the flowers blooming, as if life were threatening to overtake her when she knew it was death that was the encroacher. The grape vines grew lower, entwining with the boughs of the willow chairs, as if threatening to scoop them into a cluster and throw them up to the sun to ripen, while the grass underneath fought to drown the chairs in green. I took a picture of the chairs last year in this condition but I conveniently lost it. I do have a snap of me, fifteen pounds thinner from not sleeping while Florence lay dying, and one of my Mom at Flo's wake, crying like she couldn't at Ruth's. Maybe someday I could frame them and hang them and still be able to walk through the room, but I doubt it. Right now all I can manage is that first snap of the two empty chairs. My friends don't understand it. Nor do they understand why I'm borrowing a truck and calling around for a hack-saw.

"I have to save the chairs," I tell them, slamming down the phone on my mother and dashing for my jacket. The house has been sold, finally, my mother tells me, and the new owners are sure to throw Wren and Rudy's chairs into the dump—if there's anything left of them. They were nearly part of the grape-vine forest last year when Florence died. First thing in the morning I'll cut the chairs away from the underbrush and drive them to a field near Bolinas. They can sit together and watch the unruly grass grow up around them, again.

SOLSTICE

•
SOLSTICE

I don't generally celebrate Christmas but I am hanging six stockings next to the television set, decking the boughs with the best of them. I sheepishly wonder if anyone will think I am ridiculous.

My lover Arnison, a very reluctant participant in the festivities, has been told that this isn't anti-feminist: this is a Solstice celebration. Both of us know, however, that it's some kind of bastardized Jesus-day, a masquerade of something matriarchal, something material, yet filled, for me, with quite another set of topics—thoughts of my mother, children, and the baby I don't seem to have.

I *do* have two daughters, of sorts. I am a woman, married to the mother of two adult women. Today I am running through the house trying to give them the kind of Christmas I always had as a child. It is a particularly strong drive for me this year because the voice of my own mother, the image of her, is so close to my shoulder that it's as if I have to dodge out of her way. It's as if *she* is the one scurrying to pack and festoon, to indulge the girls in all the tremendous tension of surprise, games of hide and seek and 'who does the box belong to?' My mother wrapped us up in new scarves and hats and the things we needed, as if Christmas were a time to lavish protection on us, to take ordinary things like underwear with the price tag attached, and turn them into special kinds of care.

Today, however, I feel a bit ridiculous because the last presents to be wrapped are two ducks, little stuffed animals that bounce up and down on elastic strings. They quack. They're precious. They are not, however, for girls the age of Arnison's daughters and as I frantically try to wrap them I don't understand why I have bought them. In the kitchen Arnison is, sensibly, making the kids' favorite caviar pie while I stand with two boxes far too small for the contents, and these childrens' toys.

Arnison's daughters are in their twenties and I am in my thirties, ages so close that I cannot really call them my daughters. No one on the street would believe that introduction so I cannot use co-motherhood as a simple way of explaining who we are, what the dynamic of the moment is, why we might be out shopping together on my plastic.

They are too old for the kind of mothering a beginner like me can pull off with finesse. They're too old to be held and stroked, thought adorable, scolded and, frankly, parenthood just doesn't seem real without that era of slobber and bedtime stories.

They're full-grown women, and yet still in need of mothering (as we always are) and they look to me, a woman who is their mother's lover and so not their mother, not their father, not really their friend.

And I'm not interested in being just their friend, just someone who could come or go. Since reaching my thirties, I have developed an intense and painful desire for a daughter: I see little bitty redheads on the street and start crying. For two years I have gone through one of these crying jags nearly every single day, sometimes more than once, driving on the freeway with the tears pouring down my face while I think of a daughter reaching up to be held.

Despite my urban life, my free and easy childlessness, I have discovered a part of me that believes adulthood involves an Evinrude outboard motor, two daughters in the prow and a bucket of blue gills. I want to be able to say, hands on hips, "Listen, I have two *kids* to send to college," spoken with that fierce loyalty and determination that women have towards their children. I can hear my mother saying it--"I don't care *when* visiting hours are over, that's my *daughter."*

But my behavior is inappropriate, badly timed: I cry in diners when a little girl reaches over to stick a bit of cracker in her mother's mouth. Arnison doesn't remember the feeling. She says "Gretch, Gretchen, you're crying over spit-covered crackers?"

I know the theory that if children were considered part of a global community, women like me could be more involved with them. There's got to be another way to love a child than by *making* one—such an excessive measure, seems to me. Arnison is always saying, "but Gretchen, motherhood is an oppression," and I agree, but I think that the denial of motherhood is also an oppression, that cutting someone off from all contact with children is debilitating, as is the isolation of a mother with her child.

Well, I understand the theory, but it doesn't stop the cravings for a baby. Clearly, I am not convinced, since I have purchased stuffed animals for women who would prefer stereo components. I sit down next to the Christmas tree with the little ducks, and despite my feminist refusal to believe in the "fulfillment theory" of motherhood, inside me is a place that has begun to ache again, an emotional muscle that is not being worked. I and women like me longing for children don't talk about the desire for something, dreaming about a way of life—we talk about a pain, a loss. I don't honestly know if I want a child: I just know I have intense pain over not having one. Without a daughter, my life stretches out as an ugly stereotype: the childless spinster buying strange things for her niece, being too close to her dog, too fussy in her house, picky about her food and the way things change. Ultimately, the woman without a child, no matter how deeply she is loved, is seen to be pitiable.

The pain of living without a child is worsened by the tenuousness of other facets of my life. So much of what I have is a combination of "is" and "isn't" : I am married to a woman but the state does not consider it binding; I am a fiction writer forced to work at what she pretends is a business career. Both of these precious items—art and my relationship—are dependent on the sheer force of my will to preserve them, despite a lack of acknowledged structure. With motherhood, as well, I am left with a fragile connection, a bond no stronger than the relationship I have with my lover—after all, if Arnison leaves me, she takes my family as well. And if I acted on my theory of the global parent, my relationship to children would be no more permanent than the attachment to little strangers in a daycare center. It would give me motherhood that ended at 5:15 when the child clambered into someone else's car.

The formlessness of this life doesn't seem like freedom from role models anymore, it feels like being cut adrift, like living without the guarantees that others take for granted. We didn't grow up that way: You can hate her, adore her, disown her, worship her, wish you never knew her but your mother is your mother and I've never met anyone capable of living without that relationship.

I suppose I have a very close approximation to motherhood. I talk to my friends about "the kids", but my ears hear this uncomfortable combination of a true feeling and a strange situation so I have never called the kids this to their faces. Somehow it feels dishonest, as if I had an ulterior motive: I think, 'My God, Gretchen, why would Arnison's daughters want to be your baby-substitutes?'

And frankly, I have seen Arnison's ex-lovers grow distant from the children and I wonder how much difference it makes to the daughters. Those women are not their mothers. And if these women are not the girls' mothers by association with Arnison, then I'm not their mother either and that makes me very sad. Arnie says "Write another book Gretch, you'll be a grandmother soon enough," but the mathematics doesn't work for that any better than for motherhood—who at my age can call herself a grandmother in public. I've begun to plot towards the day anyway: I've already got the baby's library started. Maybe I could be the godmother, I think, though I haven't told the daughters this scheme, either, because I think it seems a bit devious: wouldn't they feel terribly used, as if the agenda for the baby wasn't their own?

I know I'm not alone in this predicament: I have met other lovers of mothers who struggle for years to be accepted as a parent in the eyes of a hostile sixteen year old boy, a rebellious heterosexual daughter. I meet them in the bars and at the festivals, these patient, courageous co-mothers who are dedicated to building a family when they're the only one in the situation without permanence. A co-mother starts in the middle of the continuum of a child's life and if she's lucky enough to have a granddaughter, gets to go back and live the beginning.

Of course none of this is to suggest that I'm equipped to deal with the realistic aspects of motherhood. Arnison, poor thing, is just recovering from motherhood so the prospect of a pregnant significant-other has her shaken up. Her tactic is to point out these realities. She says, "You know, Gretchen, if you have a baby, that's the end of your wardrobe: have you ever seen spit-up on silk?"

I believe her, because like so many women these days, I know nothing about being a mother. No one ever pressured me or presented it as the ultimate fulfillment. I haven't held a baby in my arms in, easily, 15 years and there isn't a child under drinking age that knows me by name. Arnison's daughters and family life came as quite a shock. Therapy has taught me about equality but traditional motherhood teaches women sacrifice, so when the daughters moved back into town and landed on our doorstep, preferring to watch horror films to my re-runs of I Love Lucy, I didn't know how to act. It never occurred to me to say 'no.' Mothers on commercials never say 'no', but what about all that goddamn therapy? I honestly was left with a battle inside myself and not a clue to its outcome. I thought, 'Whaddaya mean, we're paying for pizza *again*: Motherhood is scraping strained peas off little cheeks, it's little bibs with giraffes on the front. Motherhood is not picking up the check and stocking the fridge.' Blindly staring at the TV for some kind of clue, I thought, 'Christ, who would *do* this motherhood thing?'

Today, on Christmas, looking at the stuffed animals I have abandoned by the tree, I realize that through all my longings I really just want to love these two women. It strikes me as very simple and yet unsettling. Perhaps the little stuffed animals show me that I'm relying on artificial aspects of motherhood to bring me this love: the false connections of the chain of command, documents, and who pays for school. I am trying—too hard, perhaps—to make them into my daughters, to fabricate a depth of love as if it were something you could cut out of magic cloth. The potential for love that already exists between the three of us is frightening enough: How on earth could I find the courage to just call the two of them up, I think, and ask them out for dinner?

The question makes me see that my desire for children is as much to receive love as to give it, as much to have these daughters take me into their hearts as to take them into mine. It may be clear to mothers that you pledge never to leave the child so that the child never leaves you, but non-mothers and those of us teary-eyed on the middle ground, don't think that perhaps *we* are the ones that want that certainty again, that a child may be a safeguard against our own abandonment.

I certainly offer that to my mother. No matter what, she is my mother and conversely, she has given me not only a childhood filled with tremendous passion, but real devotion, despite enormous troubles and differences. Today, at Christmas, she is palpably here, moving through my little apartment, dancing in her stocking feet to Bing Crosby Christmas carols. It is partly for my mother that this entire celebration is planned. Arnison and I have sent her a huge woolen shawl with a card that said, 'Something to wrap you in our love,' something to protect her in return for the scarves and underwear she gave me.

Mother entered a rehabilitation hospital just before Thanksgiving and members of my family consider it the end of a very long drinking spell. Despite my studied, 12-step caution, my heart's reaction is like the impulse to buy stuffed animals— appropriate or not, I am bursting out happy. My mother is sober. I have missed her tremendously. Before she entered the hospital, her best friend told me that she was dying. Truly dying this time. I have been preparing for her death since I resigned myself to her drinking. The only thing I hung onto was astral projection—a ridiculous daydream that as she died she would appear to me, ghostlike, and say, "Gretchen, I am happy. Really happy." I could disregard the imagined auto accident: she had chosen to go and was finally at peace.

Since my mother went into the de-tox program, I have felt myself with her, at *her* shoulder. In this other-world drama, I lie in the hospital bed with the IV needle in *my* arm, I sit in a robe by the window, staring at the leaves, wondering what to do next and how to approach it. I am the one feeling proud and yet not quite sure how to continue.

But she has continued, is conquering it, and is here in spirit. Today, my mother is moving in and out of me; I am her as she hung our stockings full of fruit, she is me exclaiming over the smell of pine. I am the joyous side of my mother and my heart is jumping around the house with the best gift I have gotten in years—my mother's sobriety.

There are ribbons and bows on my heart today— corny, unsophisticated, like so much else of this mother-hood and daughterhood stuff, but still bells and holly. I am not their mother but I have two daughters coming to receive their gifts and, while she never really left, my mother has returned.

Today, there is a woman inside myself I have never met, and she is mulling the cider, sensibly putting away the stuffed animals for a baby shower, boxing the shirt the youngest will need for New Year's Eve, an appliance for the eldest, presents, like the ducks, given with the desire to wrap these women up and hold them, show them a Merry Christmas that comes from this mother inside myself, and from the beauty of my own mother, two women so visible, and yet not seen.

GIRLS FROM A NOVEL

GIRLS FROM A NOVEL

Two Portraits from
On The Job Distractions

ALEX

Lousy coffee and a greasy donut: Hurray for Mondays, Alex thought, slamming her shoulder against the sticking glass door. Lunchtime, and she was back to work with the same damn stuff she ate for breakfast. She wasn't safe on the streets anymore.

She was crazy to think a walk to Market Street would clear her head when the printing press had been slapping at her ears all morning. Alex was still haggard from the night before but she had gone for lunch anyway, crossing the intersections with dragging feet, passing the liquor stores and the dry cleaners. The walk started out alright. She took a deep breath. Just as she started thinking it was safe to be out and about, she passed a pizza parlor.

The last time Alex had seen Bettina they had been in a pizza parlor with bright lights and maps of the New

York City subway on the walls. It was late and they were both wearing heavy eyes, their big coats over pajama tops and sweat pants. Bettina rarely dressed up for her anymore and tonight she sat sideways to the table, staring at the wall, hardly eating. Alex leaned over the pizza platter, chomping on big pieces of crust, her elbows stretched into the middle of the table.

"Com'on baby, eat your pizza," Alex said.

Bettina flashed her a look, stared back at the wall. A table-top video game beside them was flashing and making phrases with its electronic voice.

"Hey, it's talkin' to 'ya, Tina," Alex nodded at the game.

Bettina glared at her lover, then cupped her chin in her hand and turned away.

"Hey, you don't know," Alex said, setting down her slice. "It could be sayin' something very important. I mean, it's just trying to talk to you."

"Shut up, Alex."

"That is Bingo-Bongo Gulch over there."

Alex watched Bettina's eyes trace the route from Manhattan to Queens, up to the Bronx, to Brooklyn to Queens, Manhattan, up and back, time and time again. Alex had little clumps of red-sauce sticking to her cheeks and rice flour clinging to her bottom lip. It had been like this for days—Bettina not saying anything, sitting despondently on the living room sofa as if waiting for a bus.

Alex turned away: she couldn't watch Bettina, engrossed, as if planning her escape. She stared at a woman leaning on the front counter.

"Hey Tina, you like that dress? Padded shoulders, tight around the knees, the whole bit. Huh? You want me to get you a dress like that? No, you don't like red. Well, how about a blue one? You'd look beautiful."

Bettina turned, sighed, set her hands on the table, her forehead tight between the eyes. She was silent.

"Doesn't matter, baby," Alex said. "You look beautiful anyway," and leaning almost into the platter, her nose touching the lino table and the crumbs, Alex kissed Bettina's knuckles.

Every night since then, Alex closed the door to her apartment as if she were putting the last brick in a dam. She threw her jacket onto a chair and went into the bedroom, sat on the edge of the bed to untie and kick off her shoes. There was no sound in her apartment and no noises in her head. She spent the rest of her evenings staring at the floor, feeling sick and hollow and exhausted, as if every night she re-lived the moment when she came home and found the note on the floor beside the bed. 'It doesn't work, Alex, and I can't stand the fighting anymore,' and so on, and so on, full of I love you's.

And Alex, every night, stared at the spot as if waiting for another letter to appear, full of I love you's and I've thought it over, I'm coming back. Look, I'm a new woman now, the problems won't be the same; the whole universe has re-made itself, baby.

But the note didn't arrive and every morning Alex got up and came to the shop, ran the printing press, sat here at lunch still staring at a spot on the floor, her body aching for the chance to put her arms around the woman's hips and draw her in between her legs, put her cheek on Bettina's belly in its crisp cotton shirt. Her thighs struggled for the chance to be straddled by Bettina's legs, the woman's cunt riding across her flesh. Where was Bettina's hair that would fall across her face and shield her? And her breasts that could be held in a hundred ways and then lie thick and full on Alex's chest after the woman had climaxed, the sex-sweat dripping between them onto Alex as if to say I...have come...with you.

The apartment was always silent now. The fighting of the last two months had sucked out all the sound, left a vacuum, like a forest after a tornado when even the birds won't come out. "Why can't you just...don't you see that...I can't stand it anymore when you...Fuck you, you're wrong, you're wrong!! Look, all I ask is that you...What's the matter, don't you care...Who were you with...why were you..." and around and around until all that's left is "I don't care, do what you want...Never mind, you're not listening anyway...Doesn't it matter to you that I..." and finally, a note on the floor.

Alex almost never took her clothes off now, except to fall into bed and cover herself with blankets. She tried to forget the weekends naked in the kitchen, concocting dinners, Bettina at the stove, Alex standing behind her pressing her mound into her buttocks or Bettina at the sink, elbow deep in soap suds while Alex sat on the floor, her back against the cupboards with her face in Bettina's cunt. Or Alex throwing on a jumpsuit to rush to the store for wine then bursting into the apartment and pulling Tina to the floor again; naked days at the Russian River when there was everything in the world and nothing more important than to trace the tiny gold hairs along Bettina's belly.

And look at me now, Alex thought. Sitting here staring at the shop floor when she should be working. Alex had run from the pizza parlor, back to the liquor store, with nothing for lunch but more coffee and another donut. There wasn't any way to reach Bettina. Friends wouldn't tell her where she was, so Alex was left with mental pictures of Bettina in another woman's arms, a vision of theft, of breaking and entering, these other women not even seeming like women: Bettina in a wombat's arms, Bettina kissing slugs. It wasn't fair. Alex couldn't even be on the streets anymore.

Alex opened the little white sack and stared inside. She'd never get any work done on a stomach full of donuts.

BECCA

In the darkroom on the other side of the building, Becca hesitantly pulled another negative out of the developer with a pair of tongs, the liquid sheeting off into the tray. Without a grey scale or a timer she would have to decide for herself when the negatives were developed. She had stood in the corner of the darkroom staring at the pile of work to be done for half an hour but there was no avoiding it—she would have to make the decisions herself.

Becca dropped the neg into the tray and held another up to the red light. Was it ready? She couldn't decide. Just like last night when she couldn't make up her mind, couldn't stay and make love, couldn't say no with finesse. Jesus, can't everyone see I'm a new dyke, she thought, I must wear it like a sign. It's a wonder the woman had asked me home.

Becca had come out six months ago and she had seen perhaps two cunts other than her own. She was just getting to know where everything was, let alone what one would do to make a woman throw her head back and groan. Well, it was something no one ever discussed, she thought, throwing the tongs into the tray, wanting to pretend to be sick and leave work. She couldn't just walk up to someone and say, "Hey, I just came out and I don't know how to...well...I mean, how do you...go down on someone...exactly?"

All Becca had ever heard was that 'a woman knew how to please a woman' and that lesbian sex was great because you made someone feel the way you felt. Nice talk, Becca thought, but that assumed you were born with the knowledge. Looking into the tray again, Becca realized she had waited too long: The negatives had gone completely black and she would have to start over again. Well you couldn't find stuff about sex in the movies, Becca thought, and it wasn't in the literature except a line or two about the first kiss and then something about coffee in the morning.

Everything last night had gone haywire. At 10 o'clock she had clambered onto a barstool and was immediately engaged in conversation by a woman next to her, someone much older with teased hair and a polyester blouse. Becca nodded and murmured, was polite even though she didn't want to talk but knew she would anyway, to avoid feeling as if she was in a carpool with everyone staring straight ahead, pretending to be alone.

They had been talking for a couple of hours when Becca raised a finger for another beer.

"So, my name's Maggie," the woman said, putting one hand on her hip and another on Becca's shoulder. "Why don't you come home with me. I make a great Eggs Benedict."

"Um...I'm a vegetarian," Becca said softly.

Maggie mouth dropped open a little, then she smiled.

"We'll take good care of you, sweetie. Now where's your coat?" She clasped the young woman by the elbow and lead her out the door.

At Maggie's place, they sat with highballs on tie-dye pillows, aimlessly chatting as before. Maggie sat sideways on the pilllow like a mermaid, her feet pointing outward and her breasts pointing up, looking coy. That was when Becca realized that while she had a desire to be seduced, she would also have to do some seducing.

"Um, I can't...stay."

Maggie cradled the back of Becca's head in her hand, drew her in, kissed her. Becca unbuttoned Maggie's blouse, then brought her hand up to explore...only the woman's face, the back of her head. They kissed, slid to the floor and pressed their bodies together. Maggie unbuttoned Becca's pants and pulled them to her knees, dropping her face into her cunt immediately. Becca gasped with surprise. Her need was huge and she came quickly, too quickly, with her shirt on and her shoes on and Maggie looking up at her like the mail had just been delivered before it was posted.

Maggie brought her hot face to Becca's lips and they held each other, waiting.

No one moved. The two women lay on their hip bones with arms around backs, faces pointing in opposite directions, the sexual interest draining away like water through fingers that will not close. Finally, Maggie pulled away and reached for a cigarette.

"I can...uh...call a cab," Becca said and when there was no sound from the other woman, laying breasts exposed, face masked, she pulled herself up and searched the darkness for the phone.

Becca sat in the stuffy cab, angry with herself, her arms limp and useless like a little girl asking mother to put on her mittens. It had always been this way, waiting for mother, for someone else.

In her family, each child's laundry would sit in a specified place for her to take to her room and each child would walk by it, not seeing it, until Mother dictated, "Take those things to your room, Rebecca." Suddenly there were socks there.

On family vacations little Rebecca would be dressed in what her mother called 'nice, sensible' clothes— a skirt with pleats that needed to be sat on just so, the creases straight beneath her legs and a gauzy white blouse that buttoned in the back where she could not reach. The car whizzed down the freeway with Becca sitting primly on the back seat, staring at the clouds and the sticks of telephone poles. Life, motion and direction were like the car speeding beneath her: she went somewhere, but she was taken. "No dear," her father had said, "I don't need to teach you to change a tire. Just stand by the car looking pretty and someone will take care of it."

And that was what Becca was taught about her body. Attract, Rebecca and leave the rest to someone else. But a lesbian doesn't live like that, Becca thought today. Everything depends on her ability to *make* sexual excitement, not just *be* sexual excitement. Good slogan for a poster, she thought, but knowing it doesn't help on a Thursday night at Amelia's.

"Don't touch yourself, dear," her mother nervously told the twelve year old girl who sat on the toilet. The woman put on her mascara before going to Dance Club. "It's...well, it's not *good*," she said and sailed out of the room. Rebecca was a good girl. She always did what she was told. Her mother never mentioned sex again so she didn't touch herself again. Not for seven years. She would take hot baths, like her mother instructed. She would go out with boys and let them touch her but that was *them*. That was someone doing it for her, to her; she never again explored herself. When Rebecca had been bleeding for a year and learned about tampons in the locker room, her mother told her crisply, "No. We don't buy those. Only *bad* girls put things inside."

Only bad girls, Rebecca had thought. The tampons she insisted on buying wouldn't go in. Her mother wouldn't show her, her girlfriends wouldn't touch her and she was told not to touch herself. Only bad girls, she thought and her cunt closed up and she started to sweat. She told her mother in a half-whisper, "there's something wrong." She couldn't get it in, but she couldn't say that she hardly knew where it went.

"Well, if it's that important to you, dear," her mother replied, "we can send you...to the doctor."

Rebecca had sat in the examination room, perspiring into her nice flowered blouse. This was important, but it was horrible. Dr. Bench, her hands on her hips, tried to talk about 'other problems' Rebecca might be having with 'her body,' to avoid acknowledging that she was there for something so simple. Dr. Bench held the skinny tube of sterile white cardboard, smeared with lubricant.

"You just put it *in*," she said, and shoved it into the blushing girl. "Then you pull it by the string," and yanked on the dry plug. She unwrapped another and smeared it up. "Here. Now you do it."

Today, in the darkroom, Becca couldn't remember the outcome of the doctor's visit. It had felt so much like last night, so much like waiting for someone else, her hands useless at her sides. Had she inserted the tampon in front of Dr. Bench? She didn't remember: all she could recall was being paralyzed at the words, "Here Rebecca, now you do it."

A FAVORITE HAUNT

A
FAVORITE
HAUNT

The steam from Abbie's plate of veal rose into her face as she bent in awe at the perfect swirls of sauce, one buttery yellow, one creamy brown, each contained to its side of the plate and spotted with tiny carrots, not a drop or speck outside the chef's design.

Abbie lifted her face to me, the gold caps gleaming on her teeth, her eyes warm, but tragic like a child who's found her favorite stuffed turtle after a good, long cry.

"This is why I love coming here," she said, a flush rising to her lined face.

She gave this speech every time we ate at Chez Nous, a French restaurant that seemed an oddity: all this brass and crystal in an industrial neighborhood, a part of town where solvents blew in the air at noon. Chez Nous had tremendous food, a gay staff and prices we used to consider outrageous. After Abbie's first monologue on her love of this place, I thought she was justifying a couple of working-class dykes blowing all their money on a fantasy. I guess I didn't know Abbie very well.

At that first dinner, fifteen years ago, we stepped through the heavy oak doors of the restaurant as new lovers. It was my birthday and I wore a turquoise lambswool dress, cut down the back to the crack in my ass. She seemed to like it. Abbie had only slept with me once and she kept watching the French neckline of the dress as it slid further and further off my shoulders, threatening to fall into a puddle around my thighs. I grinned a little but pretended not to notice the cloth's meanderings, or Abbie as she watched the rise and fall of my breath. I had shopped for hours.

Abbie looked away from my collarbone, ordered wine. We fiddled with the linen napkins, admired the artwork and the tapestries. Our manners were impeccable—and acquired—since we had both come from backgrounds of Malmac and silverware you ordered through the mail—four box tops for a knife and fork. Table manners were learned like a second language.

My desire for Abbie had been building all day and was now being fueled by gate-crashing the upper class and the sound of the voices at the table next to us. While we held hands between the candlesticks, murmuring sweet things about wanting each other, a priest, a couple of monks and some laywomen discussed the Book of Revelations. The voices carried in counterpoint.

"And Jesus said unto the..."

"Umm, baby, I can smell your skin over here..."

"And bringing the lambs and fishes to the sacristy..."

"When can we fuck, gorgeous, now?"

For an ex-Catholic, it was heaven on earth: the most wicked and dangerous situation. I thought, 'Com'on Goddess, make my dress fall. Let me reach under the table and unzip her pants.' Abbie bit her lip and clutched her wine glass.

Then they served dinner.

We began with plates of escargot, four big shells in an oily sauce of pesto and garlic, the smell of it nearly coating my cheeks. I talked of Abbie's beautiful breasts and picked up the spring-loaded tongs made of silver, gripped the shell, ate the snail with relish, talked of her nipples, grabbed another shell. I loved her ass, I said, leaning into the table, my long black hair falling to my left side. I was engrossed, but the snail wasn't paying attention: it sprang from the tongs, spewed green garlic sauce across the front of my dress and whizzed over my right shoulder. As it shot out through the restaurant it passed several tables and finally skidded to a stop in the middle of the floor, puddling its goo into the carpet.

Abbie broke into laughter that was loud, from the middle of her belly. I turned to see the waiter deftly bend and scoop up the snail in a napkin, everyone but Abbie and I pretending that nothing had happened. That's just what she wanted, Abbie said, someone with style who wasn't *too* middle class.

For dessert at that first dinner, we fed each other chocolate mousse and poached pears. We had fallen from lust into love.

The second time we ate at Chez Nous, it was our fourth anniversary. The evening had a very different feel.

Abbie and I spent an hour or more bellied up to the downstairs bar. She growled over the menu: upper class people spent this much money just to avoid doing the dishes, she complained, no point in buying what she could cook at home. She went to restaurants to sample the unusual, the exotic, she muttered and I thought she made eating out sound like going to the zoo.

We ordered wine. Our conversation was lax and surly. There was no mention of sex, no hint of seduction. We argued over the dishes, the children, whose job was worse, whose mother had been less loving. As I became simpering to placate Abbie, she became vicious and loud. Our voices began to make people's heads turn. Plates of non-descript food arrived but we continued roles so deeply memorized that there was no need to even consult our minds. She shouted, I grimmaced. The first course had arrived and the others were waiting, leaving us nothing to do but sit like spectacles and finish. That night was our fourth anniversary but I don't remember what we ate or what we wore. There was no chocolate mousse or poached pears: we would have knocked each others' teeth out with the spoons.

In the weeks following the disastrous anniversary we turned our heads away when we drove past the restaurant. We didn't speak about the evening until weeks later.

"Do you suppose we did that on purpose?" Abbie asked, making a right turn to avoid the street. "Making fools of ourselves at the restaurant?"

I stared out the window, finally turning towards her at a red light.

"What's the matter, Abbie, don't we *deserve* to be happy?"

Both of us stared ahead as if seeing the terrain for the first time.

"If we make it to our fifth anniversary, let's buy our therapists champagne," Abbie said.

Abbie and I began to make a passionate discipline of avoiding the past. When we weren't re-learning it, we were trivializing it, running from it, boxing it up as if it carried the virus of our relationship's destruction. If you exorcise the past, we reasoned, you exorcise the problems. We tried anything that held the potential of a fresh start. Abbie and Ruth ate chocolate, Abbie and I ate dried fruit. Susan and I drank coffee, Abbie and I drank tea. I wore nothing but denim with Susan so I took everything blue to Community Thrift. This relationship with Abbie was going to work, I chanted, and if it took grey shirts to make

sure, grey shirts it was. To save ourselves from the fate of
the past, we left town on the weekends as we had never
with anyone else; we cooked dinners together as if stew-
ing the cement that would hold us together. Never again,
Abbie had grumbled, as she put a timer and a rationing-
chart on the TV set: it was television that had ruined their
love, she breathed, it must have been the television.

The past sometimes followed us around. Even
after four years, Abbie's ex-lover would occasionally appear and create a dull pain in my chest. The look on her
face made it clear she had loved Abbie very much and as I
looked at the woman, I wondered about my future, ques-
tioning if I, too, would lose, even though I, too, had loved.

Abbie and I bought champagne for our therapists
several years in a row and on our 10th anniversary, went
back to Chez Nous. That night, we took up both "our"
table and the one that had seated the priest and his study
group. We had grown into an entire clan of women.

Abbie busied herself checking up on her oldest
daughter and her grandchild, turning then to her youngest
daughter who leaned against her girlfriend and two
daughters. Abbie's oldest sister, who had moved into an
apartment down the street and a deep space in my heart,
was catching up on the news with my best friend and her
girlfriend.

The plates arrived on huge trays, spewing forth
every smell a kitchen can offer. Soon we were elbow deep
in our favorite sauces, arms reaching for the butter, the
cream and a bit of someone else's food, the salt, or a knife,
while across the table, a hand cupped a smiling cheek.

The people surrounding us were part of the way
Abbie and I had learned to take ourselves and our relationship very seriously. We spent our time clear-headed,
working. Working on talking, caring, working on securing our money, our jobs, our children's future, buying
things for our house, making things legal and permanent,
drawing comfort and stability towards ourselves as if

taking tiny pieces of life and love and battening them down.

We drew people to us in the same way: cultivating a friend here, developing a new relationship with our families there, securing them to us for their love, to give them love, to share the warmth. And when the world scorched us, or the 10 o'clock news was bad, Abbie and I would walk through our house as if trying to collect all our efforts and draw this tarpaulin over us for protection, the two of us huddled under it for the heat.

That night, after the girls went off to their East Bay flats and our friends out to the bars, we went home and made love, an event whose rarity was not troublesome. We touched slowly, carefully, offering solace and tenderness and a familiarity that years ago we had disdained and now had grown to count on. We had learned to allow each other a very private space in sex, not the insistent clinging of newlyweds, but a tempered assurance that if either floated off into fantasy, she would return. The other was happy to be part of the send-off.

Tonight, years later than even that anniversary, we are here at Chez Nous, alone, having given and taken and convinced ourselves that daughters and granddaughters always come home. It is our fifteenth anniversary and the mood is bittersweet.

Our life is sweet but our best friends, who were also together for fifteen years, have just broken up. One of the bonds of our friendship with them has always come from crossing the same milestones at the same time. If it just happened to them, was it going to happen to us? All day, Abbie's eyes have alternated between fear and sadness as she talked nervously about what the early signs might have been, what the symptoms were, trying to convince herself that early detection can guarantee a cure.

"Do you think they were each too wrapped up in their work?" she asked me as she finished the last bite of veal and pushed the plate away.

I didn't know. If I had thought it was just a fear of breaking up that was making her ask, I might have tried to calm her, but fears of all kinds had been building in us for several years. It seemed that just when we had finally secured our home and family, we had become more afraid of life. Just when we had gained power over our circumstances, we had begun to feel powerless in the face of fate. Five years ago, the phrase we uttered was "when we finally get"...but now it was " what if suddenly..?"

I suppose after 50 years of watching television reports on snipers, earthquakes that strike without warning and the inevitability of nuclear destruction, it was sensible that we should feel this way. But through all the uncertainty, somehow love had escaped the ravages of our growing fear. We continued to work hard and somewhere inside ourselves, where women nestle unreasonable beliefs, we carried the hope that a couple could pass the milestone of a magic number of years and then never have to worry about it failing, again.

Breaking-up even sounded adolescent; it was for youngsters who needed to figure out pussy, or pretend they didn't need or want to be needed. It just wasn't supposed to happen after fifteen years.

"I didn't hear anything about another woman," Abbie whispered. "Do you think Sybil met someone at work? I mean, they just couldn't have...gotten bored, do you think?"

I didn't know the answer and the question gave me a knot in my stomach as if faced by yet another young woman who expected me to have all the magic answers on relationships. They asked us breathlessly, "how many years?" and sometimes I couldn't bear to tell them. They would repeat the answer like an incantation— *"Fifteen"*— and then immediately look at me with skepticism. Their next question, either silent or spoken, was always, "yeah, but is the sex still good?" or "My God, have you *always* been monogamous?" Then they'd sit back and wonder:"Wow, you think they're still in love?"

The waiter poured us coffee and Abbie looked up from her cup with the same question in her eyes. Such a basic change in the scenery, such a challenge to her foundation as the break-up of our best friends had thrown her ego back to age 20, despite her beautiful silver hair, its shock of white from the forehead. She just didn't want to accept that unlike all our stocks, our state retirement plans and money market funds, there is no maturity date on a certificate of love. The working class girl simply could not go down to the bank and check the balance.

"Maybe they closed their channels of communication," she pondered.

I took the last bite of my salmon and pulled my coffee towards me. The waiter was there immediately to clear the plate. My darling just did *not* want to hear that there is no FSLIC for bankrupt relationships.

I stirred my coffee, a little weary thinking of the relentless work of a relationship, the constant vigilance of it all. I preferred to block those thoughts with dessert questions and the taste of salmon in my mouth.

"You never, ever doubt us, do you?" Abbie said, falling back in her chair and wrapping her fingers together.

"No," I said, then turned my head away. "Not for years."

"I don't know whether that's reassuring or not."

I pushed aside my coffee and took her hand, pulling it to my face. I kissed her knuckles, rubbed my cheek along the back of her hand. I had nothing to say, no fine print that would explain it all.

"Abbie, can't the warmth of a favorite haunt be worth the chance of it burning down tomorrow? Never to cook another poached pear?"

"Now don't get abstract on me; I'm talking about terrible pain, here."

"What happens if the most precious thing in the world comes without a guarantee?" I said, not knowing if it was true. Did you puzzle together pieces of a life with one woman or try a series of women only to remember each one with a smell, a song, an income level? How can so many of us live here and still have no geography of love? I had absolutely no answers, not even a neat, catch-all-but-explain-nothing-philosophy that might serve to change the subject at parties.

But I did know that if Abbie put her cup down and walked away tonight I'd try again. Still without lights, maps or a handrail to steady me, I'd be back, haunting the same old place of love, the terrifying possibility of joy. I'd glide around the edges of devotion and companionship, in my desire for love like an old ghost that can't be shoo-ed away with broom or sticks or flailing arms.

Abbie sighed deeply and dropped her hands. "Do I have you, baby...hook, line and sinker?" she asked me, her eyes finally settling into the age of her face.

"With the rowboat *and* the summerhouse, my darling."

She sighed, flashed me those gold caps, then eyes that looked happy, maybe a bit resigned.

"Alright, alright," she said softly. "Waiter, we'd like two snifters of warm Cognac, please. And do you have mousse tonight? Maybe pears? Alright. One of each, please.

"Great restaurant," she said to me, stretching her hands across the table. "A very nice place."

NORE
AND
ZELDA

•
NORE
AND
ZELDA

Eleanora pressed her shoulders against the side of the barn, holding the thick braid of hair in one fist, the hedge shears in the other.

She squinted against the searing afternoon as she looked around the corner of the barn at the men filing past her uncle, their faces blurred and their gestures exaggerated by the heat baking off the yard. The farmhands shook the dust out of their hair and slapped at their pantlegs while Uncle Jack, hay still clinging to the back of his shirt, wiped the sweat from around his neck and handed the next man in line a packet of money, then reached into a box and pulled up a pint of whiskey. The workers folded the money solemnly into a pocket, grabbed the whiskey with anxious hands and made it the subject of jokes.

Eleanora leaned back against the barn. She clenched the braid tightly in her fist until it made her palm itch and sweat as if she held something alive, something demanding the freedom to slither under a rock. She was as dirty and covered with hay as the men; she wanted to wash the grit from her own face. She wouldn't join them though—she was family and she was a girl. But she wasn't family. Word of it had been hissed in her ear today, the sting of it smarting her burned and dirty face.

"You're just a field hand like the rest of us," the man had said scornfully as he tipped back a jug and let torrents of water run over the sides of his mouth.

Eleanora turned back to watch the men jostling each other nervously, as they held the pints and tried not to scratch at the shafts of hay that had flown into their shirts and the waistbands of their pants. The haybaling was finished. Eleanora herself had been on the top of the wagon, as she always was, working as hard, as long, as well. In the fields the boys would joke with her but away from the wagons they'd suddenly feel distant, look puzzled, as if she and they were somehow different when they laid down their pitchforks. Eleanora, every night, would sit on the porch until they had finished washing, then go to the trough alone.

Today, though, even the porch didn't feel safe, she thought, as she looked down at the braid hanging in the dust. Earlier that day, she had come to the house to rinse some of the heat out of her bandana. Across the porch, two of the girls who did the baking were combing each other's hair, lost in some dream of soothing strokes and the shine of hair dried in the sun. Eleanora watched their little motions, the way they touched an ear, a cheek; Eleanora watched them quietly as if beneath nesting birds. The girls never looked up. What was their life like, Eleanora thought? She had braided her own tangled rope of hair herself and it had fallen across her shoulder more times today than she could tolerate. She had never been a girl like that, never been touched like that before.

Eleanora had stood on the porch feeling dirty and torn, a scarecrow in comparison to the girls in their pressed frocks and smooth hair. The only dirt on either of them was a tiny smudge of molasses clinging to the wrist of the youngest as she slumped dreamily against the swing with her hand dangling over the armrest as if it had never had anything to do.

Eleanora wasn't a girl like that, and yet now, with the men streaming towards the trough to wash off the day's dust, she didn't feel like a field hand either. She had come back to the house when the men began their procession but seeing the porch swing where the girls had been, couldn't bring herself to enter. Wasn't she was a member of the family? Adopted, but a member of the family. A girl at least?

As the men lined up for their money, Eleanora had run to the tool shed, slammed the door. Seeing the hedge clippers, she took them from the wall, glaring at them as if they could cut a pattern, a definition into her life. She hacked at the thick yellow braid with sawing, tearing motions, her tears and her hair falling onto the front of her shirt.

Now, with the ends of her ragged hair flapping in gusts of wind, Eleanora turned away from the line of men and walked the barnyard slowly, mezmerized, as if she had been enlivened for a moment, then left once again chilled and silent as after a storm.

She had not begun here, on the farm. Eleanora was born in Chicago in 1895 on a day of celebration, with noisy children banging tin and hollering under her mother's window. Eleanora, though, was quiet and still. Even at five and six years old, her life was silent, making little impression on her mind except the sound of the door closing in the morning when the light was pale on the wall beside the bed, opening in the late afternoon when the light was warm. She was certain she had spent time with her mother but somehow could never remember the woman's arm around her or the feeling of her cheek against her mother's breast and, though she often tried, she couldn't remember the woman's face in much detail.

Eleanora told herself this wasn't particularly upsetting. She understood the burden the woman (she always called her mother "the woman") had lived under. The only recollection she had of her mother was holding her hand as they stared at a stranger, "Aunt Mildred," in a buggy, the day Mildred McAleer drove to Chicago and took Eleanora to the farm, leaving no trace of her mother, no mention of the city.

Eleanora, the oldest girl and the only one adopted, grew up surrounded by children fed on solid answers. Wide-eyed, the other girls looked up and saw Mother. Eleanora looked up and saw questions. No one provided her with answers. She grew up with a fog around her, a thin mist that obscured her understanding of what she saw, kept her passive and silent. She sought explanations in the birds migrating from the trees by the creek, mornings that smelled of flour, the odd shape of flies dead in the cream at the top of the pitcher. She asked questions of the plow horses resting at the top of the hill on Sunday afternoons, wondered at the feel of the pump squeaking under her own, strong hands. Eleanora was raised by the hayfields, the gold lawns stretching to the trees, the pattern of wind across the field in S-shapes and double Z's. She watched, in the late spring, the wind punching at the stalks of hay like a boxer, hitting the field in five places at once.

She was the supreme haymaker. Eleanora lifted, tossed and spread the hay with a rhythm, swung a fork all day like a man, counted the conical heaps of hay in the field and came closest to the number of bales it would make. She paced through the field with this man she called Uncle Jack, her hands behind her, him clutching a pipe in his mouth, both of them watching for weeds, calculating in their mind how much, what price, sometimes pretending to decipher when they were simply reciting their work and their patience like a long, slow stanza. At the end of the season, like today, she stood on top of the hay wagon, catching on her fork great bundles tossed into the air.

Eleanora was a big girl by the time she was 14 and after puberty seemed to put on more muscle. She never thought about her size and no one else on the farm did either; Aunt Mildred had put her into knickers and white shirts almost from the day she had arrived because a quick perusal told her that there wasn't a girls' dress in the house to accomodate her. It seemed sensible, the woman had reasoned: they were miles away from anyone so the girl could change her clothes when company came or she went into town. Eleanora grew up with the sleeves of her white shirt rolled up around her biceps and her cotton britches cinched tight around her waist, quietly lost in the mass of children and work to be done.

Today, Eleanora wandered the barnyard with her shorn hair and a mind full of fog despite the sunshine and heat. She took her braid to the corner of the property, looked down at the dusty ends of it, the twigs it had gathered from the ground. Now she wouldn't have any-thing to brush, any reason to sit on the porch swing at all. She flung the braid as far as she could, watching it twist through the air and disappear into the bushes. Slowly, quietly, she walked to the trough to wash for dinner.

Aunt Mildred set down a plate of yams. What on earth had she done with her hair? Boys' clothing was fine for work, but now the girl wouldn't be presentable even for going to the store.

"It got in my way, Aunt Mildred," Eleanora said quietly, picking up her knife and fork. Mildred stared at the child, then passed the serving spoon to her husband as if asking for an opinion. Jack dug into the yams without comment and Mildred sighed: with four daughters and five sons of my own, she thought, this one will have to make her own way in the world. Mildred took off her apron and sat at the end of the table.

After dinner Eleanora walked the edges of the fields as she did nearly every night, sometimes with Uncle Jack, usually alone. Pacing over the wagon ruts with even, methodical steps, Eleanora walked to the far ends of the field where she could look back and see the house, small lamps burning in the rooms, sometimes hear the family closing doors, hauling buckets and tubs. Tonight she ran a hand through her ragged hair, feeling as if she could stand in the field for hours and not sense the dew that was dampening her jacket, not even understand that the sun going down meant night. There had to be a place away from the sleepy patterns she had lived in, simply planting, then waiting, then hoeing it under. There had to be a place where she could wake up from this pain. It was more acute when she stood in the dark, in the cool night air and saw it from a distance. No one had ever touched her like those girls touched each other. No one had ever stroked her or lightly tickled the back of her neck while putting a thong around the mass of her hair. She had never sat in the sun...to feel pretty. There had to be someplace she could do that.

Eleanora resolved to take the train eighty miles north, back to Chicago.

Uncle Jack was in the kitchen with an empty cup of coffee when she came in from the field.

"I want *my* money, too," Eleanora said quietly. Jack looked up from his cup.

"Your money?"

"If I'm a field hand, I should be paid like a field hand," she said.

Jack regarded her cautiously, then got up and went to the pantry where he pulled a packet of money from a tin box.

"I'm assuming you don't want the whiskey."

"I'm going to Chicago, Uncle Jack."

Jack looked at the floor, pushed his hands into his pockets.

"You be sure to tell Mildred. It would hurt her pretty bad if you didn't say goodbye."

Mildred McAleer had blanched when she heard the girl's decision, then puzzled for hours over the idea of Eleanora among city people: what to do about her hair? People were more accepting in the country, where practical attire had its own value, but in the city there would be little leniency towards a broad-shouldered girl who lumbered around in britches. How could she teach the child to walk properly at this late date?

Mildred and the girls fussed over Eleanora for hours, measuring her, tailoring blouses, combing, assessing, debating this jacket and this second-hand petticoat, never really including Eleanora in the discussion, but being attentive like never before. Mildred's eyes had filled as she took Eleanora's hand and faltered over her words: get a buggy directly to the place recommended by the church auxilary, the New Chicago Hotel for Ladies. Give them money for one week and look for a job first thing the next morning. Food was not good in the cities, Mildred said, and Eleanora would have to work hard to afford the vegetables she took for granted around the farm.

Eleanora listened, puzzling over the tears in the woman's eyes. When she was packed and started down the road to town where a wagon would take her to the train, Mildred and the girls watched as if marveling at the odd stripes of a retreating animal.

Eleanora arrived at the New Chicago Hotel for Ladies with a small bag of clothes and her first hat, carried in her hands like the heaviest burden she'd ever borne. Skirts of navy blue cotton slapped around her ankles and dragged on the side, showing the pointed toes of shoes that hurt her feet. Stepping out of the taxi, she gathered the skirt in her fist like so many unruly blades of hay, and stopped at the ten-foot windows of the Chicago Bazaar next door to the hotel. They were stuffed with brass picture frames, linaments, eyelash curlers, glass dolls with ten different dresses, lamps, licorice, soap and boxes of pills. The Bazaar was like a month of visits to the farm-town store, Eleanora thought. Next door, sleds and carts and little wagons piled outside the shuttered doors proclaimed The Chicago Baby Buggy Company, and in No. 14, Henry Siede's Furs, the window was decorated with hats and shoulder shawls with the little animal's feet still on, ladies' coats fur-trimmed inside and out, pelts that in the setting sun shone like copper.

The New Chicago Hotel for Ladies wasn't as grand as the building for the furrier and the Chicago Bazaar. It didn't have fluted columns or flowered designs etched into the cement around the windows. It was a plain brick building with three stories of shuttered windows and two dormers poking out of the roof.

Women were lounging on sofas in the lobby when she entered. They stood in clusters and talked together as they climbed the stairs. Eleanora conducted her business in faltering sentences, never turning from the woman at the desk, feeling the back of her neck grow hot with fear of the women. Could they see she didn't belong in shoes like these? In skirts, even? Every whisper was a woman who knew she had worn pants all her life, every other sound someone laughing at her hair. When she got her room assignment, she dashed up the stairs two at a time and closed the door quickly. Why had she left the safety of the farm? There at least she had a purpose, she was the best. If she couldn't talk to the girls on the porch, why on earth had she come someplace where there were so many of them? She didn't belong with women, that was part of the problem. She hadn't the first idea what to say. Eleanora took off her skirt, threw it in the corner and climbed into bed.

The next morning, Eleanora woke with a start, anxiety driving her out of bed. Aunt Mildred had told her to get a job right away so Eleanora put on her best white blouse with lace and pulled the blue skirt from yesterday over her wide thighs.

Bounding down the stairs, she realized she was the only one up this early in the morning and, looking around for some sign of life, Eleanora saw a notice on the wall. "Help Wanted: Chicago Equity Corporation."

It took over an hour of walking and numerous requests for directions before Eleanora got to the office. The Equity Corporation was in a huge brick building with vaulted windows and gilded bears guarding the doors. As Eleanora walked across the polished floors to the reception desk, she wondered what an equity corporation did and what her job might entail. A man in a blue uniform directed her to an office at the top of the stairs.

When she opened the door, though, she stopped, puzzled. There were four other women there, though the doors could only have opened minutes before. They sat stiffly on a large sofa, staring but not seeing an older woman in very proper dress sitting at a desk.

"May I have your name, please?" the woman asked.

"Eleanora McAleer."

"Take a seat. The typing test will be given in just a moment."

"Typing?"

"We have the finest new equipment here: no complaints from our typing pool. Now, just take a seat beside the other girls, there."

The women on the couch shifted without moving their eyes from the wall. The woman sitting closest to her looked at Eleanora from under the brim of a hat bright with ribbons. The other women were those small-waisted, tight-lipped girls, Eleanora thought, like the girls in town who seemed able to suck themselves into rigid little lines. She didn't know how to type; maybe the woman could offer something else.

"Excuse me, Ma'am."

"Take a seat. We'll get to you."

The woman with the ribboned hat turned and gave a little grin, motioned with her eyes to Eleanora's hair. Eleanora cleared her throat, put her hat on and tried to push her hair into it. The young woman crossed her legs, turned and put her elbow on the back of the seat, covering her mouth with her hand.

"Now hold your hands in your lap," she whispered to Eleanora, who stiffened, then did what she was told.

"Right. Cross your legs. No, no, at the knee."

The woman at the front desk looked up from her papers.

"Alright, we'll start on the left. You, dear."

"Yes ma'am," Eleanora said.

"Where were you last employed?"

The ribboned hat whispered, "New Orleans."

"Uh, New Orleans, ma'am."

"And how many words per minute do you type?"

"Type, ma'am?"

The whisper came, "25 per minute."

"Oh, well, 25 per minute."

"I see, and where can we reach you if necessary."

"Well, I just moved into..."

"I see, well...and you, Miss, where were you last employed?"

The ribboned hat turned towards the desk. "I was an executive secretary to the Treasurer of the Mobile Trust Insurance Corporation for four years, Ma'am. I take dictation, file, of course, type 35 words per minute, handle telegram requests and personal organization. I'd be happy to show you references, naturally."

Eleanora watched the woman as she talked. She had seemed easy and natural while she whispered into her hand, but when addressing the woman at the desk, had suddenly gone stiff and proper like the others. What most astounded Eleanora, though, was the way she was dressed. The other women were in pastels with lace here and there, little jackets over their arms, gloves with tiny pearls on the clasp. This woman wore black, a close- cut black skirt and a short jacket that stopped at the waist, a white blouse with small, severe tucks down the front. And a tie. A man's tie. Eleanora couldn't take her eyes off it.

"Excuse me, Miss," the woman at the desk interrupted, pointing her pencil at Eleanora. "This is a private interview."

Eleanora glowered. How could it be private when she was sitting right there? The other women stared straight ahead as if forbidden to hear. Bad enough she had to sit there in these stupid clothes amongst all this lace and high fashion but nobody was going to treat her like a child. She may not know about the city but she certainly knew when she was being insulted.

"I think it's more than my eyes that are in the wrong place, Ma'am."

"Fine," the interviewer said. "And you can go, too," she waved her pencil at the neck-tie.

The woman in the ribboned hat slammed the door behind them.

"I'm sorry," Eleanora said, when they reached the street. "You shouldn't have to leave just because I did."

"It's not your fault. She started with our side of the couch for a reason, you know."

"What reason?"

The woman didn't answer, but walked to the main intersection with Eleanora.

"I can't get trussed up like a monkey to make a living," Eleanora said quietly.

"It's just a game, don't you think?" the woman said. "Rich, conservative people like to hire rich, conservative people, so you pretend." The woman took off her hat and her black hair fell to her shoulders, curling just as it hit her collar bone. "I don't know very much about the city," Eleanora said, "but isn't that...a man's tie?"

"Yes. You like it? It's all the rage in New York and this one's really a man's. I got it from a friend of mine, this boy who looks as ridiculous in men's clothes as...well, anyway, I just love to sit in those stuffy offices thinking 'if they only knew where this tie has been,'" she laughed.

"Anyway, good luck finding something." She touched Eleanora's arm and strode towards the intersection.

"Hey," Eleanora called. "Thanks for the help."

The woman waved a bare hand, put on her hat and turned the corner.

Eleanora wandered through the streets. The places hiring women were staffed by tight-waisted types and Eleanora couldn't bring herself to walk in the door anymore. When she found jobs she could do, she looked in at sweaty men with blackened forearms or with wood shavings clinging to their pants. She knew that the threshold of the door was her boundary.

Every day, the formlessness tightened around her until it forced Eleanora back into her room. She had less of a feeling of belonging than when she was on the farm. Her money was running out. Four days into her search, Eleanora lay in her white shirt and britches, sleeping in the late afternoon. A door across the hall slammed, waking her with a start.

"'From the remotest time,'" a woman's voice pontificated, "'man has tried to rule her who ought to be comrade and colleague.' No, Zelda I will not shut-up. You should read this. 'Every protest against this law was a women's rights movement and history contains many such protests.'"

Eleanora cracked open her door and peeked out at a woman with one finger in the air, her other hand cradling a book.

"Ack, I don't care Ellen," said a second woman whose back was to Eleanora's door. "Any book on the modern women's movement that doesn't include C.P. Gilman is *not* a modern book."

"Zelda, there *are* important contributions made that don't come out of the mouth of your beloved." The woman looked up and saw Eleanora's eyes, grabbed the other woman by the arm.

"Good...afternoon," the reader said. The second woman spun around and Eleanora, though only half visible, tried to back into her room to hide her britches and white shirt, her collar open to her cleavage and her hair mussed from sleep.

She grabbed her skirt from the bed where she had thrown it earlier and struggled into it, opening the door for fear of missing the only contact she'd had in days. Looking up at the face of the second woman, dressed in black, she stepped into the skirt and tore the opening.

"It's you again," the woman in black said, taking off her hat and letting her hair fall to her shoulders. "My name is Zelda," she said, extending her hand. The reader looked at the glow on Zelda's face, looked at Eleanora, and closed her book.

"Eleanora McAleer."

"Ellen Olsen," the reader said. "Pleased to meet you. You just get in?"

"Monday."

"Oh, Ellen," Zelda moved to Eleanora's side. "We had quite the amusing little run-around with the employment office at Equity earlier this week. Come in, come in." Zelda grabbed the skirt that Eleanora was still struggling to clasp. "Don't worry about that. I'll fix it." Eleanora let the skirt drop, as Ellen leaned against the wall and folded her arms. "Please," Zelda said, "come in."

Ellen straightened her hair. "Oh yes, I'll fix it," she mimicked under her breath.

The three went into the room, Zelda throwing her hat on the bed and lighting a lamp. Ellen plopped herself on the bed and Eleanora moved cautiously to a chair on the far side. Zelda relayed the story of the Equity Corp. as she fussed in the room, opening a window, undoing her shoes, pulling up another chair and propping her feet on the bed. Zelda and Ellen grew silent. Eleanora felt as if she were being examined, her biceps, exposed by the rolled-up sleeves, her thighs, belly, forearms, legs, the ruddy color of her neck and chest.

"I hope you're not offended by the pants," she said, "its just that on a farm..."

"You look great...very nice," Zelda said.

Ellen gave a sidelong glance at Zelda, then got up. "Well, I'm off. See you at dinner Zelda?"

"Yes, of course. We'll come and get you."

Ellen frowned at her friend, gave a little smile and a wave as she closed the door.

"Where are you from?," Zelda asked.

"Country. Near here. I was a haymaker. We had a lot of acreage."

"You look strong. I've always thought that was very...admirable." Looking at the woman's muscular forearms, Zelda's nostrils flared slightly, a little grin tugging at her face.

"Admirable," Eleanora laughed. "Well, it might be 'admirable' in the country but it isn't getting me anywhere here."

"Maybe you're just looking in the wrong places, Elen...could I call you Nore, or maybe Nora. Somehow Eleanora seems so lacey and old-fashioned."

Eleanora circled the room looking at posters and newspapers Zelda had pinned to the wall.

"You're a ...suffragette?"

"And this," Zelda said, walking to her dresser and pointing to a framed poster, "is Charlotte Perkins Gilman, the finest theoretical thinker and writer of our time. Her book <u>Women and Economics</u>, have you read it? "

Ellen stuck her head in the door again. "Has she launched into you about CP, Eleanora? Don't listen to her. There's more than one mind in this movement. Come on you two, we'll be late for dinner and you know how the boys fuss if they have to go into the hall by themselves."

"Oh God, it is late," Zelda said, grabbing her bag. "Nore, will you have dinner with us? It's not expensive and maybe we can come up with some work for you: I'll bet the boys know a trick or two. Grab another skirt and we'll meet you downstairs."

Fifteen minutes later the women were rounding the corner of 10th St., Zelda in the middle chattering about occupations for their new friend. Two young men leaning on a wrought-iron fence across the street joined the human chain on either end.

"Here you are. I just can't stand it when you're late, Zel, and who is this?"

"Bertrum, meet Nore," Zelda said. "And this is Louis."

"Charmed," Bertrum said, doing a little curtsey.

"We're just trying to conjure up a good job for Nore," Zelda said.

Bertrum threw back his head. "Well, when you find the recipe for employing a misfit *do* let me know, won't you?"

"I thought you liked it at the dry goods store," Ellen said.

"The fashions are so boring lately," Bertrum said. "You women are looking so dowdy—nothing but black and white and little jackets."

"You long for the day of the whale-bone corset and ruffled neckline, Bertrum?"

"Oh yes, there were bright colors and ribbons and..."

"Well, then you wear them," Ellen said.

"My dearest," Bertrum said, walking backwards to face Ellen, taking her hand to his cheek. "Then you give me your permission?"

"Alright, alright you two," Zelda shushed them as the group passed the theater and joined the stream of young people headed for the narrow stairs to the Ladies and Gents Dining Rooms, the third floor of the Oyster Saloon at No. 28.

"What do you think, Louis?" Zelda asked when they sat down with their plates of beef and potatoes.

"Well, Danille and Sons Haberdashery needs someone."

Ellen looked at him scornfully and Zelda snorted. "I don't really think she's the type to sell clothing, Louis."

"Well, what type is she?" Bertrum cooed.

"How about Sol. Feinber's Antiques?" Louis continued.

"You don't understand boys, this woman wants to *work*, not babysit the passerby," Zelda said.

"My, my," Bertrum rolled his eyes, "perhaps she should try the stockyards, then."

Ellen dropped her fork. "Absolutely not."

"I'm very good with livestock," Eleanora said, encouraged.

"Don't even think about it, Nore," Zelda said quietly. "Bertrum, you pig."

"Alright, I'm sorry," he said under his breath. "You don't want to do that, Nore. It's brutal."

The hall was a large open room, table after table filled with noisy diners. Nore noticed more than one group of women dressed in bright colors and low-cut dresses, women Aunt Mildred would consider of 'dubious morals'. The boys seemed either very threadbare or delicate, like this Bertrum and Louis. Maybe the food really *was* bad here in the city, though her plateful was certainly adequate. There only seemed to be one real gentlemen in the entire crowd and he, stout in his doublebreasted suit with round lapels, was striding in their direction.

"Well, Miss Zelda. Good evening dear," the gentleman said to the startled group. "Do we have a newcomer to our party?"

Zelda stiffened, then gestured formally. "This is Eleanora McAleer."

"Evening," the man nodded in her direction, then took Zelda's hand and drew it to his lips. "Scouting on train platforms are you, dear?" he murmured to her knuckles, kissing them lightly.

Zelda's face tightened, her eyes squinting in anger.

"Nore, this is...Mr. Henry Collier."

The gentleman saluted to Nore. He bowed to Ellen and kissed her hand slowly, with relish, then backed away and disappeared down the stairs.

"My," Bertrum said, circling his spoon in the air, "we are certainly being bold tonight, aren't we?" He glanced sideways at Ellen, who face was bright red as she sat clenching her purse and her coffee cup.

Home from dinner, Eleanora crossed the floor to her room in the dark and lit the lamp on the small table by the window. Zelda followed her, tossing her bag onto Nore's bed.

"I can't believe that woman," Zelda said, sitting beside her bag, her back to Nore. "Wearing that get-up in the dining hall."

Nore had gone behind her screen and had changed into her farm clothes. She threw her skirt on the floor, kicked the shoes into the corner, and stepped into the room in her chamois-colored pants and a clean white shirt.

"I'm sorry if this offends you but I can't wear that stuff anymore today," Nore said sheepishly. She sat nervously at the far end of the bed.

Zelda turned on the bed to face Nore, whose gleaming skin contrasted with the white shirt. In those clothes, she looked whole, Zelda thought, she looked graceful, as if suddenly the parts of her body knew how to move.

"You just have to be very careful, Nore. That woman tonight was taking a terrible risk."

Nore scowled, confused. Zelda looked at the door, thought about running to the safety of her own room, wondered why she was there.

"The man I introduced you to, Henry Collier..."

"The one who kissed your hand."

"Yes. Well, he is a woman."

"He was wearing..."

"A suit, that's right. And that's why we thought it terribly brazen of her. Everyone in the dining hall knows her, but as a woman. She wears that get-up to work, do you understand? She's a very bright woman and there just isn't much of a market for intelligent women, particularly ones who are fat, so..."

"I've never heard of such a thing..."

"Well, you mustn't breathe a word of it, not a single word," Zelda said, standing up and putting her hands on her hips. "You know how apprehensive you are about wearing your pants in your own room, imagine how much danger she's in."

Zelda gathered her things to leave and picked up the skirt to be mended.

Nore, Zelda and Ellen shared morning coffee in the hotel lobby, then rushed off in different directions, Ellen to her job as a telephone operator in a brass foundry, Eleanora and Zelda in search of jobs. Both the prospective employees came home, day after day, with nothing for their efforts but crumpled newspapers and dirty hemlines. Eleanora sat quietly staring at the fireplace, increasingly nervous about renting her room while the money dwindled from her bag. Zelda paced the floor.

After two weeks, over a glum cup of morning coffee, Ellen suddenly sat up as if poked.

"The Trinity Building, Zelda. They must have at least 15 companies crowded in that place and they're all doing very well—based on the traffic in the street anyway. Maybe there's something Nore can do there," Ellen said.

"And maybe the insurance companies need typists," Zelda said dubiously.

Thirty minutes later they got off the trolly in front of a five story building that housed The Pennsylvania Coal Company; E.B. Ely and Co., Shipper; the Kansas Colorado Gold Co.; Atlantic Mutual Insurance; W.B. Smaats, Attorney at Law and, monopolizing the top two floors, Hatch and Co., Lithographers. Zelda squeezed Eleanora's hand and they parted on the stairs.

Eleanora climbed the five flights to a Dutch door, the kind that opened on the top. The din of the print shop met her with a wall of sound. Men in black pants and white shirts stood in front of cabinets, pulling out a myriad of drawers and setting individual letters into trays in their hands. Presses whirled and clanked on either side of them and occasionally a young boy would wheel a rolling dolley loaded with crisp, white paper across the floor. The smell of gasoline and ink wafted over Eleanora's head.

A man approached the door, wiping his balding head. He set his ink-stained hand on the top of the half-door and leaned against the jam.

"What can I do for you, son?"

"Excuse me?" Eleanora asked, unable to hear.

"I said, what do you want, boy?"

Eleanora was dumbfounded, then looked at the door. Clearly, from his angle, he couldn't see the skirt she was wearing. Her face grew hot. She thought about standing on top of the haycart with her muscles flexed and warm.

"A job, sir."

"What?"

"A job!" she shouted.

"You a printer?"

"No sir, but I'm strong," she shouted.

"You honest? I can see you're strong."

"What, sir?" she shouted.

"Alright, we'll start you hauling paper, tomorrow."

"Excuse me?"

"Tomorrow! Damn if you're not the biggest kid I've seen through here in years. Seven a.m. We'll talk wage after you work," he shouted. "What's your name?"

"Nore."

"Norm?"

"Nore!"

"Alright, Norm, seven a.m. and I don't need to tell you that in this place, you be prepared to work!"

"Zelda! Zelda!" she screamed, tearing up the stairs two at a time, her skirts up to her knees. "I'm taking you to dinner."

Zelda threw open the door to her room.

"I got a job!"

Zelda shrieked and Ellen came out of her room, full of congratulations.

"Finally! Finally!" Nore said. The three stumbled into Zelda's room, and Eleanora paced as the others fell onto the bed.

"I really didn't know what I was going to do."

"Where? Doing what?" Ellen said, sitting up on her elbows.

"In a print shop. Hatch and Co. I waited for you, Zel, but I didn't know which office you went into and I was so excited I ran all the way back here. I couldn't remember which tram we took."

"A print shop?"

"Yeah. Tomorrow I haul paper. That's what they're going to start me on." Nore looked at the perplexed faces. "I guess they think I'm a boy."

"Nore," Ellen admonished quietly.

"Well, this man talked to me across a half-door so I guess he didn't know."

"Oh my God, Nore," Zelda said.

"It was noisy and when he asked my name he thought I said 'Norm.' You know, like Norman."

Ellen started laughing and fell back across the bed.

"I want this job, Zelda," Nore said.

"Well, you should keep the job, then," she said.

"Zelda," Ellen said, standing up to pace the floor beside Nore.

"Seriously," Zelda said to Ellen. "If they think she looks like a boy like this, wait 'til they see her in drag."

"It is very dangerous to impersonate a man," Ellen said with deliberation.

"Only if you're caught, Ellen," Zelda countered.

"Well," Ellen murmured, reconsidering. "I suppose she is a prime candidate, isn't she?"

Zelda rummaged in her drawers for a pair of scissors.

"Now wait a minute, Zelda, you can't just mold Nore into what you want her to be," Ellen protested. "When the chips are down *she's* the one who's got to carry it off."

"I want this job, Ellen," Nore said quietly, watching the women discussing her like the girls did with Aunt Mildred before she left the farm.

"Zelda, you can't make an innocent into your loving husband just because you want her!" Ellen said.

"Why not? Then we could double-date, eh, Ellen?"

Ellen put her hands on her hips, her face reddening. "Help yourself dear," Ellen slammed the door behind her.

"What is she talking about, Zelda?" Nore asked quietly.

Zelda held the scissors and looked at Nore. How could she not see who she was surrounded by? Could Nore really be that innocent, that unknowing? Her body radiates vitality, it announces her, but her face seems oblivious, unaware of what lies inside or beyond. Could it be right to give her body the challenge of passing when her mind was so clearly unprepared? How could Zelda tell her about lesbians, when Nore had no point of reference for anything but pitchforks and wagons? Zelda turned away, went to her dresser and set down the scissors.

Looking up at her posters of C.P. Gillman, Zelda felt very alone. Her excitement over Nore's job had gone and she felt attacked, invalidated by the woman's naivety about lesbianism, threatened by her possible reaction. Even the need to explain herself offended her. Especially when she felt a deepening attraction for this woman whose tanned skin at the neckline of her shirt called out to be touched.

"We're lesbians, Nore."

Zelda crossed the room, hoping to hide her own fear and vulnerability. She took Nore by the hand as she would a child and sat down on the bed to explain.

Later that evening, Nore sat on the edge of the bed, her hands folded between her knees, a deep crevice in her brow. Zelda was pacing the room. The explanation had not been difficult, since Nore was like a blank page that needed no correction, a clear space for Zelda's information. But Zelda felt agitated, hurt by the necessity to explain her life in such detail, frightened by the risk she was taking. Nore had said very little.

"I didn't ask you," Nore said, breaking the silence, "did you find work today?"

"No," Zelda said tersely. "I didn't."

"I don't understand it," Nore said, "with all your experience."

Zelda stopped in the middle of the room and threw up her hands.

"I was never anybody's secretary, Nore," she said, irritated. "You think I would get a job in their prissy little offices if I told the truth? I'm a fishmonger's daughter. I know fish, Nore, not typewriters. I know John Dory and lingcod and periwinkles." She leaned on her dresser.

"Skate. Catfish. Cabezon—I'll bet you've never heard of that one, have you? I've worked with knives since I was 10 years old and let me tell you, you get used to your hands being in guts all day. My mother and I had a stand on the dock where the customers on the pier bobbed up and down one way and the dock rolled in the waves another way, like kids on see-saws."

Zelda threw the curtains open with an upward sweep of her arms, then let them fall and turned back to Nore.

"You want to know why I don't care what the world thinks of me? Because every night walking home with my mother, the sidewalks would clear from the smell of us."

She sat on the bed.

"You give me a sharp knife and I can slice fish so pretty a rich girl would think it *swam* without bones. But where would that get me in this world, do you think? Being rich is a game, Nore, that's what I tried to tell you the first day we met. You can live whatever you can play.

"So I decided, alright, if being rich means pretending you're too fragile, too pure for things like fish then I'll play the game. I'll cross my legs and fold my hands across my little lace cuffs and tell them how refined I am. They'll make it a reality, Nore, because it's true, you can live anything you can play."

In the morning, Nore lay in bed wondering if she was the same woman. Zelda had trimmed her hair carefully, struggling to find a cut that would look mannish when slicked back with pomade during the day but womanly enough to not arouse suspicion in the boardinghouse. Zelda had clipped and stared, walked to the side and clipped a little more, moving back and forth in front of Nore, her skirts rustling close to Nore's face. Zelda had run her hands across Nore's temples, her fingers combing, then smoothing the hair onto her neck. Zelda had worked for nearly two hours while Nore sat speechless, watching the flicker of a candle burning on the dresser and the movements of Zelda's skirt. When she seemed to be finished, Zelda cupped Nore's face in her hands, tilted her chin upwards, then moved behind her and put her hand along the left side of Nore's face, held her protectively, set the scissors down, then, without a word, opened the door for Nore to leave.

Nore walked to the Trinity Building, comfortable in her favorite black pants and white shirt, uncomfortable in her hidden identity. After leaving the boardinghouse in a skirt, pants underneath, Nore darted into an alley to slip off the skirt and stuff it into a paper bag. She stepped back into the street with hesitation, expecting the traffic to stop, crowds to jeer or push her off the sidewalk. Instead, people moved out of her way. Men walked with her stride, at her shoulder, as if she belonged in their group. Hawkers asked to shine her shoes and sell her newspapers. It was as if she were suddenly in a completely different city, a town of greater riches. Nore glanced to her side as she moved down the street. People who didn't try to sell her something ignored her completely, as if she had suddenly become invisible. They didn't look her over as they did when she walked in her skirts. Nore stuffed her hands deep into her pockets, the paper bag stuck under her arm.

"Alright, Norm, this is Mickey," shouted Mr. Henry, the balding manager, as he brought the two together. "There's a shipment of paper coming in the elevator. Stack it on those roll-away pallets. See the ...."

"What?"

"I said see the man with the mustache, Norm?"

"Mustache..."

"John...the foreman. You got questions, ask him first, then me..."

Nore nodded and went with Mickey to the gated elevator.

"Must be the fresh air makes those country boys so hairless," someone shouted above the din. Nore stiffened and glanced at Mickey, who either didn't hear the remark or didn't care. When the paper arrived, he simply motioned to the other end of the box and the two began their day of work.

With the first motion of her muscles, Nore felt her spirits lightening. Just to be moving again, working, the feel of her body doing something with which it was familiar. And to be making some money, she thought. Who knew if the charade would fool anyone but maybe if she kept her head bent and worked she could make it through just one day to get paid.

"Alright," Mickey shouted, "wheel this load over to the biggest press, the one on the end over there. Another load's comin'."

Nore pushed on the stack with her shoulder, then maneuvered the roll-away down the center aisle between the cabinets and the presses.

"Thanks...I'm Jim," a burly white-haired man offered his hand.

"Nor...Norm."

"Pleasure."

"What?"

"Pleasure to meet you."

It was nearly dark when Nore left the Trinity Building and headed home tired and sweaty, but more at ease than she had felt since arriving in Chicago. Despite the strain of the masquerade, Nore was now living like the woman she had been in the country, a hard-working, strong-armed woman outside the world of the feminine, still invisible to men. She strolled home, too happy to sit in the tram and too unsure to be in close quarters with people. The manager had wanted Norman back in the morning, had slapped him on the back, promised him a future. Now all he had to do was find a suitable alley in which to transform into Eleanora again.

When Nore came home to the New Chicago Hotel for Ladies, a cluster of women were gathering in the lobby. She smiled at them, but the confused looks she got froze her heart and made her take immediate inventory. She had forgotten the pomade, her hair was still slicked back, her face was probably covered with dirt. Nore dashed up the flight of stairs to her room and closed the door tightly behind her, then stumbled to the bed. First one disguise, then another. She threw off her clothes and climbed under the covers.

"Nore!" Zelda whispered into the darkened room a few hours later. "Are you here?"

"Zelda?"

"When you didn't come to the dining hall I was afraid something had happened to you."

"I'm so tired. It worked, Zelda," she laughed as she sat up in bed in her undershirt, pulling the blankets up modestly. "They thought Norman was a really hard worker and they want him back in the morning."

"Oh, God."

"I don't know, Zelda, you think this will work?"

"Well, I brought you a little something to help," Zelda said.

"You sound tired, too. How did it go?"

"The only thing that kept me from screaming in the street was the thought of your hair, my dear."

"You should have seen the women in lobby when I came home."

"That's why I got you this." Zelda put a hatbox on Nore's lap and went to the bureau to light the lamp.

"Zelda, you've hardly got money for food. You city people do things in the screwiest manner."

Nore opened the hat box and pulled out an oversized beret, so large and floppy it sat in folds in her lap. Zelda arranged it on Nore's head with a peak and a dip, like an elegant sculpture or a massive bird. It hid every strand of her hair and made Nore's eyes the focus of her face. Zelda brought her hands down slowly from Nore's head, dropped them into her own lap and stared at the woman's big open face, sleepy and soft.

"I was thinking about you today," Nore said softly. "I don't know what it all means, but I was thinking about you."

"Go to sleep, dear," Zelda turned off the light and shut the door softly behind her.

As the weeks went on, Zelda became more distracted, first nervously reciting lines and tactics for interviews, then slumping into her chair, despondent. She stopped pressing the ribbons for her hat, the wrinkles from her skirt, giving up on their ability to help her. This morning, Zelda had taken only enough time to clasp on a little bracelet and it hung around the cuff of her wrinkled shirt like a talisman.

Zelda's loose dress contrasted with the fury on her face. The second and third weeks of walking through the city she berated employers, the upper class, the chances for happiness in such a world. She was surly during interviews, shouted at trucks that crossed her path on the street. Zelda was becoming more difficult to give to as time went on, Nore thought. Zelda, drawn inside her fury like a crab, was a struggle to comfort and a struggle to ignore. She took dinner from Nore without comment, since her pride stopped her from being grateful and her gratitude made her ashamed of her silence.

Nore, at first confused by the occasional sharpness of Zelda's replies, hung back. She had never tried to understand a woman as she was attempting to do with Zelda. She had never thought about Aunt Mildred's life; the girls were too young, too foreign. Zelda was a woman in dresses and pointed shoes like the girls on the porch, but a woman who could be understood, Nore thought. In between the hopeless clothing and the indignant face, Nore saw a woman who was fragile, and she thought there was beauty in such a vulnerable woman choosing to be a fighter. The woman wore her masks uneasily, as Nore did her britches and her blue skirt.

Nore watched Zelda holding the cup as if the warm tea promised comfort. The bracelet seemed shabby compared to Zelda's skin and the rounded bone of her delicate wrist. The little bracelet held none of the strength of the woman, the jewelry's steady patterns and aura of grace a mockery of the way Zelda set down the cup, touched her lips, brushed her hair from her cheek. Zelda was talking softly with Ellen, her voice straining to sound reasonable and measured, but it was that small wrist that Nore watched, as if it contained both the beauty and pain of the woman.

To Zelda, the problem was more than just a shortage of money. The lack of a job called into question her ability to play the game with those in power. Did people see through her disguise as she walked through the streets, clutching a newspaper and her small blue bag, she wondered? Perhaps she looked like a painted doll, as much a poor imitation as the mannequin in the furrier's window. She began glancing in others' direction when she walked, losing that self-assured forward gaze and the confident way she usually pressed herself through the crowd.

Zelda had been raised to carry herself well at all times. She had stood beside her mother and watched the woman use fish to tell the story her body wouldn't divulge. Her mother slipped lemon in with the lingcod for the chatty women in bonnets or the men to whom she told stories, gesturing with her knife, leaning far across the wide table's rim to deliver a punch line. When the dealing became hectic and price the only factor, Zelda's mother would fling the fish back and forth across the table, victimizing them for a penny lost here, another bargained there, the little fish bodies slapping against the sides of the trough and flinging bits of scale onto Zelda's blouse. When the crowd built around them, Zelda and her mother trimmed and gutted with precision, standing back to back yet pulled into themselves for protection.

In the summer when she was twelve, a man with a red nose had stuck his face towards Zelda from the crowd as she furiously scraped and cut and wrapped.

"It's not that one, girl, I've bought the trout," he growled. "And the lingcod. Be quick."

Zelda looked around her. There was no other fish to be cleaned. Further down the trough was a lone trout, probably set aside by her mother for the man from the university.

"That one," the man said shortly, pointing at the isolated trout. "Quick. I haven't got all day, pretty girl."

Zelda looked up into the man's face, red and veined.

A knife cut the air between them, gouging into the wood where it stayed, upright. Her mother leaned over, grabbed a handful of fish guts until her hand was bloody and covered, then threw the guts onto the table in front of the man and stuck an accusing hand in his face.

"You *ever* try to confuse my girl...You get outta here. I don't need your money that bad."

That wasn't true, Zelda knew. They needed every penny, every sale. And now that his fish was gutted and wrapped it would be harder to sell as fresh. She leaned against her mother and felt the tightened muscles in the woman's legs. The man backed up, offered his money with a grumble. Her mother took it without taking her eyes from the man, then scooped up the package and shoved it at him.

"You ever see that man again you stay away, Zelda," her mother said, "you don't ever talk to him, you don't get near him, you come straight to me and say so."

At the end of that long day, when their blue working coats were covered with entrails and scales, and her mother was carefully wiping her hands in a ritual of each finger, then nail, the man with the cap drove up in the carriage. It was the driver for a family Zelda had never seen but he came every week at this time.

Her mother, her hair wisping after the free-wheeling trade, stiffened and smoothed her clothing. With a simple nod, the two walked to the end of the dock and Zelda's mother, with great ceremony, drew back the wooden doors of a cabinet that held a huge salted salmon. The fish was nearly as large as Zelda. Her mother had taken off the head a week ago for their own soup and the dark pink flesh was the brightest color on the dock. The driver nodded. Zelda's mother drew out a very large knife from the cupboard and, steadying herself as if chopping wood, she began sawing on the massive hulk. The driver stood motionless as she cut slice after slice and laid them gently on white paper.

Her mother was perspiring and disheveled when she returned with the tall stack of cutlets and wrapped them on the table. Zelda did not look up but felt keenly the woman's discomfort. The man in front of them wore linen, with brass buttons that shone. His hair was slicked back and untouched. Zelda, without looking, could see on her own dress every mended hem and spot of fishguts, could see on the woman above her every wrinkle and cut and strand of unruly hair. Her mother took his money and folded it quickly into her skirt but as he turned to go, she reached under the table to the little plate where she and Zelda saved bits of fish for their own dinner. She deftly wrapped them in white paper.

"And for you, sir, something for your own wife and children," her mother said in a smooth and refined tone that belied her dirty smock. "From Stanley," she said, then looking down at Zelda, "From Stanley and Co."

Zelda was horrified. That was their dinner. There was no fish left. They were not a fancy 'company' that could give presents or anglers on a big boat who threw fish in the air for seagulls catch. Zelda knew they were only a plateful of scraps away from having no dinner. The man was surprised and the sudden light in his eyes made her mother straighten.

"Oh," the man breathed. "They rarely....get such things," he said. Instead of his usual stiff nod of the head, the driver offered his hand, then departed.

Zelda looked up at her mother, confused.

"Salmon tonight, Zelda," she said with a laugh, then strode over to the salting cupboard and drew out her knife.

After dinner with Nore and Ellen, Zelda went directly to bed. The next morning she walked on the streets with irritation, as if she were late, though she knew she had nowhere to go. She occasionally stood undecided, then changed directions. She growled at men who bumped into her, then drew into herself and was silent. Ellen had forced her to press her clothes and do her hair in a special way but her heart wasn't into the job search and she spun her hat in her hands, kicking stones with the toe of her boot.

Zelda went into a huge department store on the main thoroughfare and wandered through the aisles, running a finger along the glass cases, looking at the hats and baubles. Zelda felt as if it was the repository of all the things in the world she would never be able to buy. She pulled on the belts, held bottles of perfume as if they were weapons.

When she turned the corner past the scarves, Zelda stood in front of a "Help Wanted" sign on a glass case. She read it several times before waking up and seeing the lingerie section. Zelda peered at the neatly folded rows of panties, the white pantaloons and, hanging from their little straps, the rows of camisoles in pastel silks, ribbons, lace. The showpiece of the department, displayed at the corner junction of all the display cases, was the wooden bodice of a woman in a slip, the cream lace barely covering her large upright breasts. The mannequin was surrounded by flowers and huge peacock feathers, a jewelry box spilling its contents, a cup of fine china. Zelda stared at the warm color of the wooden figure, the fall of the silk. She felt herself warming inside. They want to *pay* someone to look at this all day, she thought, narrowing her eyes and grinning to herself.

"May I help you?" a woman said.

"Good afternoon," Zelda said, regaining her composure and drawing herself into a regal manner. She extended her hand. "I understand you are in need of assistance, Madam. You surely must be the manager."

"I am."

"I am Zelda Stanley."

"Fine. Fine. Do you have experience with ladies lingerie?"

"Oh, gracious yes," Zelda said, wanting to cackle and slap her leg. She talked about the job as if seducing it, drawing down her voice, rolling her words off her tongue. She talked with the woman at length but saw in front of her only the bodice, the lace, the breasts. Within the hour she was walking into the personnel office to sign the papers.

Listening in the dining hall to the news of Zelda's job, Ellen put her cheek in her palm and shook her head. The boys simply turned in their chairs and looked away.

"Bosoms," Bertrum whispered to Louis.

Nore sat very still, pleased that the search was over but curious over Ellen's knowing smile.

"Our dear Zelda," Ellen said, "fitting...ladies all day."

Zelda just sat with her head thrown back, her arms stretched against the table and laughed.

Ellen ate a last forkful of peas. "Alright girls, down your coffees, we have to go. C'mon Nore, you're going with us."

"Corrupting the innocent," Bertrum said, slapping the tabletop lightly. "Maybe she doesn't *want* to be a part of your espionage club."

"Be quiet, Bertrum."

The women coursed through the backstreets until they reached a small carriage house with a dark blue door and a brass knocker. The three were admitted to a square brick studio. Women pulled chairs from hidden corners and struggled to marshall the seats into straight lines. Other women were engrossed in a discussion in the corner. Ellen joined their group. Soon the studio was so full it was necessary for everyone to sit down to find room.

A woman in blue gabardine, book and papers in hand, stood in front of the thirty-five attentive women.

"She's reading Charlotte tonight," Zelda whispered, eyes flashing as if in some private triumph.

Ellen rejoined the group, sitting at Zelda's right, accompanied by a large woman in a brown dress.

"As to Humanness," the woman in the front intoned in a high theatrical style. "Let us begin, inoffensively, with sheep."

"Oh Christ," the woman beside Ellen grumbled. Zelda shot her a glance.

"Nore," Zelda whispered, "this is Beth Collier."

Nore looked at the woman, recognized the gentleman from the dining room. Beth offered her hand, and Nore searched the woman's face for a sign, a mole, a color in her eyes that would tell her why she had begun dressing like a man, and more importantly, how she got away with it.

"Industry, at its base," the speaker intoned, "is a feminine function. Woman became the first inventor and laborer; being in truth the mother of all industry as well as all people."

"Yes yes," Beth leaned back and put her arm on the back of Ellen's chair "but what about action!"

"Could we have it quiet in the back please," the speaker said. The women in the back of the room, leaning against the wall or sitting less demurely than the lace-clad women in front, crossed their arms over their black jackets, their tailored blue smocks, and shifted in their seats.

"In the earlier part of the women's movement," she continued, "it was sharply opposed on the ground that women would become 'unsexed.'"

The women in back laughed heartily.

"Let us note in passing," the speaker said, "that they *have* become unsexed in one particularity—the peculiar reversal of sex characteristics which makes the human female adopt the essentially masculine attribute of special sex-decoration..."

Beth and Ellen exchanged glances, laughing.

"...she blossoms forth as the peacock, in the evening wearing masculine feathers to further her feminine ends."

"Yeah!" the women in the back called out, applauding.

"Madame Chairwoman," Beth said, standing and leaning her weight on the chair in front of her, "where, may I ask, are the cookies?"

The woman in front snapped the book shut and touched the ruffle around her throat.

"Where *are* our little tiny purses, filled with our little tiny lives?" Beth said, her voice rising in tone and intensity. "We are becoming like the ladies clubs downtown—all chit and chat and *lemonade*. Our sisters in England stage..."

"The counterproductive activities of the English women make a mockery of responsibility for women..." the speaker said, setting her book down while women from the front of the room rushed into clusters at her side. The women in the back leaned forward from their casual stance, the meeting changing gears like a machine.

"Zelda," a voice beside Nore whispered. A gaunt young woman with long loose hair, a hat low over her forehead, leaned in front of Nore, then cast a glance her way.

"This is my friend Nore," Zelda whispered.

The woman nodded her acceptance. "We're planning something new. Ellen's representing you: we're meeting at the wharf after."

From the front of the room, the speaker raised her voice and stood on her tiptoes. "We *have* an action," she growled. "The Auto Tour through the State of Illinois will send speakers for street corners, continuing our drive to educate."

"In England, the women hunger-strike, here we ask permission from the town square," Beth shouted, striding into the aisle.

"It is our duty..." interjected one of the pastel-dressed women, "to support Americans choosing American tactics. Our representatives are..."

"A distinguished group alright," Zelda said, jumping to her feet and startling Nore, who had been frantically trying to follow the action. "All upper-class women and all *ladies*."

"Which is not an insulting term!" the speaker hissed.

"And who will speak from the laboring woman's viewpoint?" Zelda shouted. "The Equality League of Self-Supporting Women..."

"Which is *not* a part of this meeting!"

"...has done more to gather support for suffrage than a trainload of society ladies..."

"I move that we vote to support the Women's Autotour and begin a campaign to gather funds..." said a woman, who stepped from the side of the speaker.

"...with a provision that the funds be available only when a member of the working class is included in the line-up of speakers," Zelda shouted.

"I second the amended motion," said a voice in the back of the room.

"All those in favor say Aye," called the speaker and the room roared its approval. "So be it."

"Meeting is adjourned," shouted Beth, slapping her palms together.

"This meeting..." the speaker said icily, watching the women already moving towards the door, "is hereby...adjourned."

Ellen and Beth quickly left through a side door and Zelda took Nore's arm to lead her out the front. When Ellen returned late that night, Zelda slipped from her room into the hallway to confer. Every evening, Ellen joined the two for dinner from a different direction, suddenly breaking away from a group of women just as they turned the corner and disappeared. Nore had never seen any of Ellen's group before, except for the woman with the hat.

Nore's arms grew thick and sinewy as the weeks progressed. The work and the sweat on her forehead made her proud of her strength, but just as she felt relieved at finding a place for herself, she would catch someone's eye and quickly turn away, certain of having been discovered. She would work furiously until the warmth in her muscles made her brave again, until she was giddy with the thrill of her secret, the mystery of it enticing her to try a few manly gestures. She wiped her brow and hiked up her pants. She spit in the corner by the elevator but Mickey didn't flinch. Nore shook her head, amazed, stuffed her hankerchief in her back pocket and bent for another box. In the month she had been there, no one had had a conversation with her—talking was impossible over the din of the presses and she slipped out of the shop and trotted home before others could join her.

Nore couldn't figure it out, turning back towards the elevator. She knew how to act around men—she learned on the farm—but everyone there knew she was a woman, even after she had hacked off her hair. In the city, people were supposed to be sophistocated. How could they not know she was a woman: couldn't they see it in her face, her eyes, couldn't they smell it on her? Everything had been upside down since she boarded the train. First wearing a goddamn dress and some stupid little hat, then meeting city women who didn't mind the pants at all. It had been a horror trying to find a job, and now she didn't have to hide her pants but hide her breasts instead. She ate dinner with men who acted like women and wished for skirts, sitting beside beautiful women who slept with women as if they were men. No wonder Aunt Mildred had worried about her, Nore thought, as she heaved another box on the pile.

Nore practiced a wide-legged spread when she sat. That came easy, made her happy. She studied the stiff, arrogant walk. That made her unhappy. She slapped her bandana into her hand when she stood idle, squinted her eyes with menace when she surveyed the press room over a cup of water. She learned to pull her pant legs up slightly before crouching and cross her arms over her chest, pushing out her hips. Either the workers were too busy to notice, or, as she suspected and Zelda had assured her, they were too secure in their belief that anyone wearing the tag is the merchandise.

Occasionally, straightening up after loading a pallet, Nore would be aware of a movement inside her, a heat running through her belly and lungs that made her feel more like a woman than ever, more aware of the boundaries of her skin, and the difference between herself and the man she was expected to be. She had lived with this division in herself all her life but had never felt it as keenly as now. On the farm it had felt like a way to belong; now it seemed a cruel deception, a deception not of the public, but of her. For the first time, Nore felt as if the cloud she lived in was not a product of her own confusion but something forced on her, something held around her while she struggled to see clearly.

At these times she would act her most manly, scowl deepest and move with the most abrasive gestures she could summon, filled with fear that the self-awareness would show, that the men in the plant would see parts of her that she could only feel.

In the middle of an afternoon, while wheeling the pallet to the presses, Nore crossed in front of a thin woman in a simple green shift-dress and no hat. She clutched a small cloth bag in her hands. She was the wife of one of the typesetters and she arrived every day at this time to deliver his lunch and scurry out again.

Nore usually only caught a glimpse of her as she darted from the door to her husband who worked behind the tall wooden cabinets of type. Today, Nore was inches from her as she dashed to her husband's side and offered her little bag of food. He looked up from his work, his face suddenly creased and twisted with anger. He immediately raised a hand to slap her face, holding back from the punch just inches from her skin. She winced and Nore's breath caught short in her chest. The woman pushed herself against the cabinets as her husband brought his face close to hers, speaking in a way that made her hang her head and nod. Though she couldn't hear their words, Nore was frozen in front of the aisle. The other men, working across from the woman's husband, turned their backs on the scene and tightened their shoulders. The man asked questions with anger and the woman turned frightened eyes to him, denying, pleading, explaining. The man grabbed her arm and shook her. Nore twisted the bandana in her hand and stepped forward.

Suddenly the foreman was at Nore's side, startling her. Nore hadn't seen him coming and she didn't like him this close to her. He pointed towards the elevator and shouted something she couldn't hear. Nore turned away from the woman with the cloth bag and went back to the elevator.

Nore leaned on the wooden gate, looking down the black shaft towards the light on the first floor. There was no paper to unload when she arrived. The elevator was on the bottom floor, and the sound of the truck drivers having lunch echoed up the chamber. Nore turned around and saw the woman's hair poking above the top of the cabinet, saw her inching closer and closer to the corner. Did this happen every day? Why hadn't she ever seen it? Why hadn't she bothered to look?

Nore paced in front of the elevator. She, herself, had jumped when the foreman appeared, leaping out of her skin the same way the woman had. That's not the way Norman would have reacted, she thought. Nore had cowered, immediately, as a reflex. A man...well, a man would have looked the foreman straight in the eye. No one touches a man, Nore thought, kicking the gate of the elevator. No one makes a man grimace and cower or forces him to explain. She looked into the pressroom, saw the woman scurry away. The husband came around the side of the typecabinet and took a few steps towards Nore. She straightened, took a wide, offensive stance. He wiped his hands on a rag, scowling at her, then threw the rag on the floor and went back to his station.

Zelda ran to work in the morning as if dashing off to a rendezvous, coming home with the sheepish grin of the unfaithful. Most days she did nothing more than fold camisoles, marveling at the colors and the ribbons. Yesterday, the manager had asked her to count panties.

This morning, however, the department was busy as soon as she came in. Stock numbers and sizings replaced thoughts of women's bodies, lace on skin. Zelda had several women in the dressing rooms when a mother and her two daughters came into the department, moving with a slow elegance as if they had no destination but great purpose. They wore furs and jewels and a piece of lace tossed casually over a shoulder, a brocade bag flung about as if it were nothing, leather gloves dropped on the counter and only gathered up as an afterthought. The patterns of their skirts and coats folded into one another as they leaned together to whisper. Zelda clutched a handful of camisoles.

When they reached the rack of petticoats, the daughters became very animated. The older woman, in a large feathered hat and an imperious air, turned to Zelda.

"Miss? It seems my daughters will try on your petticoats."

The manager, talking with a customer at the end of the counter, dropped the merchandise and scurried to the mother.

"Yes, indeed. Let me get you chairs for the fitting room. Zelda?" the manager directed nervously.

The five women went into a large, curtained dressing room and the younger women began stripping off their coats and hats, flinging them across the chairs. Their mother sat down slowly. The manager bowed to her.

"This is Zelda. She will, I'm sure, help you find your fancy today."

Zelda stood in the dressing room as if she were a child again, facing women on the tram with her dress covered with fish scales and blood, this time without the security of her mother's hand. Zelda felt as if every particle of dirt that had ever touched her was now visible to these women, as if they could see how many years she had worn her first dress and how many scraps had been substitutes for dinner.

"Peach, Zelda," one of the young women cried. "Bring us your peach petticoats."

Zelda brought crinolines with lace, petticoats and bustles and slips with hoops. The women stripped down to their bloomers and cavorted in the dressing room, calling to her to bring them more. The petticoats began to fill the room, litter the floor like meringue puffs and they were still no closer to deciding. Instead, the women danced and played in the merchandise, leaning on their mother's chair and waltzing away, then crumpling into a heap on her shoes and putting their heads in her lap.

"Now girls, you may each choose one," the mother said and the girls laughed. Zelda wondered how long it would take to narrow their choices. The mother began laughing with her daughters.

"Well, Zelda, it seems that we'll just have to take them all."

"*All* of them?" Zelda asked.

The women turned their smiling faces to Zelda, hiding their mouths with their hands but drinking in the expression on Zelda's face. They hugged each other, laughing at Zelda's surprise until she stiffened, looked around at the disheveled room. Hadn't she had been roped into their game? Wasn't her surprise necessary for the thrill of their purchase? Zelda wondered in how many other stores they had looked for a fishmonger's daughter so they could buy a boxcar of stockings or chimney lamps, a coach full of gloves? Zelda's shame turned to anger as she gathered the first handful of petticoats and marched towards the register.

The manager was thrilled and the other clerks amazed as Zelda tied the last bundles of boxes together and handed them to the women. They thanked her and sailed on to another department, giggling behind their gloves.

"Zelda," the manager said, "you have another fitting." Zelda strode back to the dressing room, glad to be out of sight of the little bits of lace and silk. Inside, however, stood a woman whose plain cotton bloomers were mended and without lace. She struggled into a boned corset that Zelda, even from across the room, could see was far too small.

By the end of the day, Zelda was tired and filled with conflict. The woman with the corset had twisted and strained, insisted on Zelda pulling the straps and lacings until the bones of the corset cut into her body. Zelda nearly cried with the effort and the pain of watching her, while her heart smarted from the torment of the young women and their petticoat money.

Zelda was the last to leave the department and as she gathered her ribboned hat, the manager came to her, smiling broadly, and handed her an envelope.

"Your first commission, my dear. You did very well."

Zelda shook her hand, and when the supervisor had gone, counted the money inside. There was nearly an additional week's wages there and she held it to her chest, head bent, eyes closed. Just a little extra money. Zelda opened her eyes. On the floor near the counter, at her foot, Zelda saw a lime green chemise, lying crumpled and forgotten. She deftly bent, slipped it under her skirt and stuffed it in the leg of her bloomers. Zelda strode out of the store and towards the tram, feeling at the same time battered and blessed.

She went to her room, splayed the money across her bed, threw her clothes into a chair and slipped on the chemise. It was silk. And lace. She hugged it to her before daring to walk to her mirror. Someday she would wear silk every day, Zelda whispered to herself. And someday there would be somebody. Somebody else. She took off her stockings, slipped on a robe over the lingerie and walked to Nore's room.

Zelda walked in without knocking and stood with her back against the door, looking down at Nore who lay on the bed fully dressed, still in her hat. Zelda couldn't think of anything witty to say, anything seductive. She looked down at her bare feet. How could she finally be willing to risk it, now of all times, when all she wanted was to be held and comforted?

"Sometimes it's too hard," Zelda said softly, then covered her face with her hands and started to cry.

Nore slowly got up from the bed and stood very close to Zelda. On the farm, when one of the girls cried, Eleanora and the boys would leave the house. For the first time, Nore thought, someone was asking her for comfort, demanding something of her heart, not her muscles. Without the veil, the fog, the impermeable cloud between herself and others, Nore saw the crisp lines of Zelda's hair against her face, saw objects come into focus and deepen in color. Nore hesitantly brought her hand to Zelda's head, stroked her hair.

Zelda unbuttoned the house dress and dropped it at her feet. The silk clung to Zelda's ribs, hung lightly over the round of her breasts. Creamy lace barely concealed her nipples. The chemise hung just below Zelda's thighs, with a border of lace melding silk into skin. She pressed herself against Nore's chest, then grasped Nore's forearm and wrapped it over her own shoulder, nestling into the farmgirl's awkward embrace.

"When I'm rich, I'm going to dress like this every day," Zelda said.

Ellen tapped softly on the door, then peeked her head inside, withdrew and closed the door, then opened it again. Nore stepped away but Zelda grinned at her friend with some of the sparkle back in her face.

"We need you two," Ellen said, smiling.

"Is it tonight?" Zelda asked, wiping her wet face.
"Yes. The committee thinks we need two couples
to be walking on the train platform just before it goes off
to divert suspicion."
"Two couples?"
"Norman and Zelda, Ellen and Henry."
Zelda smiled. "Oh, Ellen, my first real boyfriend!"

The foursome walked slowly across the train platform, pretending not to notice the women from Ellen's
meeting who crossed their paths, dropped little bags of ex-
plosives into every trash bin, then caught trams out of
town. The two couples were the last to leave the platform
as it closed for the day, the ticket taker rushing off to his
dinner while Norman and Zelda, Ellen and Henry, dapper
and confident and mistaken by passersby, slowly ambled
into town for their celebration. When they were half-way
up the path to the main street, the train station exploded,
a portion of the roof scattering in all directions, benches
thrown out into the path, glass shattering onto the torn
platform. People from the streets came running towards
the rubble, bumping into the women as they stood in awe.
Zelda and Ellen pretended to be frightened, eager to be
whisked away by their suitors.

At the top of a small hill, the four looked back at
the chaos. Zelda sighed. Tomorrow the women from
Ellen's group would hang a huge banner across the torn
front of the station. "Votes for Women. Now." The twisted
planks of the building and the horrified looks on the faces
of the townspeople were another kind of justice, though,
Zelda thought. She knew that the rich women and their
petticoats had not really been destroyed, that the debris
showering down was not money to buy more silk. It was,
though, a kind of relief, as if it reaffirmed her feelings that
she could play it, she could live it and she could tear it
apart.

Nore was wide-eyed and jittery, standing with her arm around Zelda. She felt as if she were watching fireworks for her own special arrival, as if she had been given, with one explosion, a place to belong, a life to live. Nore looked around at the debris and the people running into the mayhem, looked at herself in her manly costume, standing solid and warm and, most remarkably, loved. Perhaps soon even able to give affection. Nore could hardly remember the awkward girl in the saucer hat, could hardly think why she would run from the women in the hotel lobby.

Zelda looked up at Nore and saw the change in her eyes, wanted so much to grab her by the ears, pull Nore towards her with the gesture of an elder whose heart has been caught by the brightened spirit of a child. Zelda wanted to hold Nore's cheeks between her palms and bring her close to her, drawing out the brightness in her eyes as if to find what finally made them come into the present and focus. The smoke billowed behind them, people rushed past on either side but Zelda noticed only the change in Nore's eyes. It seemed to have been a long time coming.